The B⚘⚘B Girls VII

The **B**urned **O**ut **O**ld **B**roads at Table 12

Ten Little Puritans

A Novel by Joy Johnson

ISBN: 1-56123-252-9

Library of Congress information on file.

CENTERING CORPORATION
AND
GRIEF DIGEST MAGAZINE
GRIEF RESOURCES

Order from: www.centering.org
1-866-218-0101 or 1-402-553-1200
centeringcorp@aol.com

This one is for all my "Joy Riders."
Wheelmen and women
Who drive me to presentations.

Thanks for taking great "Joy Rides" with me.

Watch for The BOOB Girls, the Musical
Coming soon to Omaha's Circle Theater.

Part One

Ten Little Puritans

Ten little Puritans dressed up so fine,
One walked on water and then there were nine.

Nine little Puritans sure they would be late,
One hurried off and then there were eight.

Eight little Puritans brightest under heaven,
One hurt her neck and then there were seven.

Seven little Puritans cutting up their tricks,
One went to sleep and then there were six.

Six little Puritans playing with a hive,
A bee stung one and then there were five.

Five little Puritans drinking in the bar,
One passed out and then there were four.

Four little Puritans up on a spree,
One got fuddled and then there were three.

Three little Puritans with a hot dog and brew,
One spilled the ketchup and then there were two.

Two little Puritans lying in the sun,
One got too hot and then there was one.

One little Puritan being all alone,
Had to run away and then there were none.

Zed Zonker was prancing . . . *prancing* . . . doing high kicks like a young man leading a marching band, his cane serving as a pounding baton. The cane hit the floor of the Meadow Lakes Retirement Community dining room in strict time to his left foot. Prance – clump – prance – clump. His physical therapist would have been proud. He wore high-top black sneakers and was waving a black top hat in his free hand, smiling and waving to an open-mouthed lunch crowd who were paying rapt attention. Zed's smile beamed under his bushy mustache, and he bounced gaily in rhythm.

Other than the sneakers and top hat, which he was actually waving not wearing, Zed Zonker was as naked as a jaybird. His aged private parts were bouncing in exactly opposite time to his prancing.

Diners in the back of the dining room were standing to get a better look. No one wanted to miss anything. Directly behind Zed, and gaining ground rapidly, was Fuss N' Feathers, the oversized rooster who ruled the Meadow Lakes chicken yard. The big rooster's head was lowered, his wings spread, his beak open, ready to grab an ankle in a chicken-like death grip.

Dashing into the dining room was the third star of the show, Sheryl, the new assistant manager at the retirement community. Sheryl's face matched the rooster's in determination and grit. She too was bent low, gaining on both bird and bare-assed man. Just as Zed turned and prance-kicked down the hall toward the elevators, Sheryl leaned forward even further and, nearly losing her balance, grabbed the rooster.

Gripping him in both hands, she crashed through the side door of the dining room and threw Fuss N' Feathers high into the air. She grabbed the door frame to keep her balance and let out a whoosh of held breath. Then she turned back into the dining room, rubbed her hands together, wiped them on her slacks and walked with great dignity down the hall toward her office. Four red feathers floated gently to the ground outside the big window.

The dining crowd closed their mouths, looked at each other and broke into thunderous applause accompanied by hoots and one ear-drum busting whistle. Zed Zonker, the chicken and the assistant manager had been the hit of the day.

Mary Rose McGill sat down at table 12 and turned toward Wiley Vondra seated at the next table. "How did you do that, Wiley Vondra? How did you get your sworn enemy, Zed Zonker, to prance through the dining room with no clothes on?"

"I crossed his hoary old palm with three hundred bucks and it was worth every penny." Wiley grinned, stood up, planted a wet one on top of Mary Rose's head and sat down again, his grin bigger even than Zed Zonker's had been.

Marge Aaron also sat back down, slid her chair up to their table and nodded her head. As the chair moved, her red cane swung back and forth where it hung on the back of her chair. "It's a good thing he didn't do that while we were having the Ladies' Flower Show."

They looked at her.

"He would have won first prize for the best dried arrangement."

They laughed. Robinson Leary raised her hand and gave Marge a high-five. Then they all looked at Hadley Joy Morris-Whitfield. She looked back at them, nodded, smiled and did a thumbs up. "Going to be a hard act to follow if we ever have a luncheon speaker," she said.

They were dressed in jeans or slacks and lightweight sweatshirts, all of a different color. They were willing spring to come by dressing in softness and hope.

Wiley Vondra wore his usual jeans and short-sleeved shirt. He had on his brown leather vest and his big Stetson hat lay at his feet near his chair.

A worried look passed over Mary Rose's face. "What if Zed gets in trouble? What if Wiley gets in trouble? What if Alphonso kicks Zed out? He doesn't like him any more than Wiley does."

"Not going to happen," a deep voice said beside them. Alphonso Greatwood, the Meadow Lakes owner, drove his Mean Machine handicap scooter up to the table and parked beside Marge. He held up an iPad. "I got it all on video. It's going on the Meadow Lakes facebook page and YouTube. If it goes viral, it will be the best advertising this place could have. We'll have a waiting list a mile long." Ever since Alphonso had purchased the retirement community, he was seldom seen without a good suit from Parsow's in Omaha's Regency Court.

Alphonso Greatwood was a retired linebacker for the Kansas City Chiefs from the time when the team first began throwing footballs. The handsome black man was still massive but no longer fast. His knees were shot beyond any hope of repair and he had been smashed in the helmet so many times he sometimes fumbled over words, got them backward and unintentionally became the king of spoonerisms.

Once, when asked about the best Chief's quarterbacks, Alphonso didn't hesitate. "Marren Woon and Moe Jontana," came out instead of Warren Moon and Joe Montana. But once Alphonso had settled in and found himself loved by the residents of Meadow Lakes, especially the ladies at table 12, by the time he found a new best friend in Wiley Vondra, Alphonso's speech improved and he was happier than he had ever been. For the first time in his life Alphonso Greatwood thought marriage wasn't such a stupid idea. He would maybe even entertain such a thought for himself.

He was still famous and every so often a sportscaster would interview him, and they always seemed to want a picture of him on his Mean Machine scooter. The oversized vehicle was painted green, had a GPS, a roll bar and a seat behind his with the words *Bitch Seat* painted on it. There were two buttons on the control panel. When Alphonso pushed one and drove forward it played the theme from the old television show, *Happy Days* because Alphonso Greatwood was the original Fonz. When he pushed the other button and backed up, the Nebraska Fight Song rang out. Alphonso may have been a KC Chief, but he hated their music.

He had purchased the one hundred and fifty retirement apartment complex from the wicked Busch family from Florida. The Busches, Thorny, Rose, Lilac and Whacker had turned the independent living community into a den of iniquity, with gambling, prostitution, liquor and an underground Viagra ring. Alphonso rescued the community and became an instant hero. He had hoped for a relationship with Robinson Leary, but that hadn't worked out and as fate would have it, he and Marge Aaron got along remarkably well.

Marge Aaron, say it fast and it's "Margarine," so she'd "butter be good." Marge was a large woman who should be large. Her gun-model grey hair was curly and cut short. She wore glasses and was thinking about getting a hearing aid. She joked, "If I get a hearing aid I can put on my glasses, stick in my hearing aid and all I need is an oxygen hose for my nose and dentures for my mouth and I'll have every orifice in my head filled with technology."

Marge was a retired homicide detective who had married a large policeman who became a cop's cop. She had given birth to two children who had also gone into law enforcement and Marge was herself, a leading detective. She had come to Meadow Lakes on contract to help solve the murder of Percolator Rasmussen, who had been found face down, spread eagled on the dining room floor of Meadow Lakes. His head had been smashed in; his throat was cut, there was a nylon cord around his neck, a bullet hole in his jacket and a knife in his back. Mary Rose McGill had been the only one to ask, "Are we sure he's dead?"

Marge had solved the murder, been instrumental in getting rid of the Busches and was still good at detecting. It was Marge who solved the mystery of the haunted bed and breakfast in Salem's Crossing, Nebraska. She also was never without a priceless accessory – a red cane. Even though she had a new knee that sometimes gave her trouble, this cane only hung over her arm, ready to be used in a different way. The red cane was bejeweled. The red cane was unlike any other. When Marge pressed one jewel it became a Taser, a second jewel turned it into a low-powered rifle, a third provided a smoke screen, a fourth spilled out tripping pellets and the last jewel saw that knives popped out of the sides. In the handle was a gold lariat, just like Wonder Woman's.

Marge wasn't a super hero, but she was a warrior woman indeed. The cane had been designed and created for her by her brother who actually worked in British intelligence where James Bond could have picked up his watch, his loaded briefcase, his car and if he had wanted one – a red cane. Robbie Leary, of all the girls at table 12, appreciated Marge's intelligence and sense of humor. She also appreciated the red cane.

Robinson (Robbie) Leary was half African American, half Cajun. Her salt and pepper hair, which was rapidly becoming pure white, framed a face the color of a rich latte. She was bright, witty and loved to study and do research. Both she and her husband had been professors at Creighton University.

Having no children or living family, they had each other and had been more than soul mates; they had been partners with Volvos and a trendy apartment in Omaha's Old Market.

Wheelchair bound from Multiple Sclerosis, her handsome husband had died in his sleep, spooned tenderly with Robbie. Staying on at Creighton and living in the Old Market seemed unbearable, and Robbie ended up taking an early retirement and a chair at table 12. Of the other three best friends, it was Mary Rose McGill who made Robbie laugh the most and whose innocence was a good balance to Robbie's professorial language and manners.

Mary Rose McGill had been transformed by the friendship she found at table 12. A sweet Catholic girl, Mary Rose had four daughters, each with the first name of "Mary." She had walked through the big entry doors of Meadow Lakes Retirement Community after the daughters had parked a U-Haul in her driveway, loaded it up and moved her without so much as asking if she wanted to go. Her suitcases and boxes had held fourteen miserable house dresses and two pair of clunky shoes because her mother had told her, "The uglier the shoe the better for your feet." But now, because the other women had seen her potential and treated her as they knew she could be, she had become that powerhouse woman – a warrior woman in her own right. She had lost weight, dyed her hair blonde and gotten red-rimmed glasses, along with an entirely new wardrobe from Target.

Mary Rose McGill had survived breast cancer, just as Robbie Leary was surviving atrial fibrillation, Marge was coping with her knee and Hadley was living with macular degeneration. All the women were getting by with more than a little help from their friends. Mary Rose had stood up to her daughters and become her own woman. Her husband, who hadn't talked to her much when he was alive and talked to her even less now that he was dead, would have been scared to death of this new woman. And she could be scary. She defended the chickens in their pen at the side yard of the complex and had even convinced a die-hard fried chicken lover that they should have privileged chicken accommodations and live well.

The fried chicken lover, of course, was Wiley Vondra, Mary Rose McGill's cuddle bunny, sweet boy and main squeeze. Mary Rose still couldn't believe that with four single women over seventy to every single man that age, someone had actually found her attractive and desirable. Wiley Vondra could.

Wiley Vondra was a Korean War veteran, a sports fan and in addition to loving fried chicken, had grown up and worked on ranches in western Nebraska. He consistently wore jeans, cowboy boots, a brown leather vest and an old Stetson cowboy hat. He was tall, thin and had a reputation for being found in the laundry room every fifteenth of the month wearing only the Stetson, boots and vest because when Wiley Vondra did his laundry, he did ALL his laundry. Wiley also did all he could to maintain his reputation. He disliked Zed Zonker voraciously and loved Alphonso and the girls enthusiastically. He was homey, dependable and had a laugh that opened a door and invited people to join in.

They had been given the name, BOOB Girls: Burned Out Old Broads, by Maggie Patten almost seven years ago. Maggie had been a rough, tough, retired Sandhills rancher who had fired five shots into her mean-talking, mean-spirited, just plain mean husband's gravestone and who had died on a short cruise off the West Coast.

Her three friends, in a raging storm, had gotten her body overboard and given her the burial at sea she wanted, even though they had all ended up as soaking wet as Maggie when she sank into the water and so exhausted they thought they might die as well.

They had loved Maggie Patten, and now they were all watching Hadley Joy Morris-Whitfield. Sometimes they watched her when they were sure she wasn't watching them. Other times they just looked at her and kept on looking.

Headlines and Highlights

It was later that afternoon and they were looking at Hadley as she leaned toward Marge's laptop computer opened wide at table 12. The mid-afternoon sun poured through the dining room windows and they were sipping decaf coffee while Hadley was reading aloud the best headlines of the year before.

Spring had finally peeked through the huge evergreens that bordered the spacious lawns. It came after a long hard winter. The last heavy, wet snow was making a weak and losing effort to keep from melting into the ground. Snow drifted down now from the sky in fits and starts, dancing in the sunlight, reminding Hadley of bunched up powdered sugar. She looked up, took off her glasses and squinted out the big window next to their table. "Snowing while the sun shines. My grandmother would say 'Snow while the sun shines will turn to rain tomorrow' I love winter when I don't have to get out, but I'm ready for a new season."

Marge Aaron looked up and nodded, "Me too, sister."

Mary Rose McGill looked out the window and shivered. "Cold. Come, Spring, come!"

Robinson Leary looked harder at Hadley. "Don't stop reading, Hadley. These are actual headlines. It names the newspaper they came from."

Hadley put her glasses back on, leaned toward the computer and squinted at the next headline. *"Bugs with wings are flying bugs,* from the Redwood California Extension Service."

The other girls looked at her.

"It gets better. Here's one from an editorial page. *Republicans turned off by size of Obama's package."*

They laughed. Hadley had their full attention. "That's a naughty one," Mary Rose giggled.

"Tiger Woods plays with own balls, Nike says."

Marge shook her head. "We are SO BAD!" She leaned as far over as she could to look at her computer. "There's the winner so far!" She read it out loud. *"Statistics show teen pregnancy drops off significantly after age 25."*

Hadley laughed. Robbie pulled the computer toward her place at the table and read the next one. *"Federal agents raid gun shop, find weapons."*

"I want one, too," Mary Rose said, sliding the computer over to face her. She scrolled up and down for a second or two. "Aha Ha! Another police report! *Marijuana Issue sent to a Joint Committee* and this one, *'February 22. Police arrest everybody.'* Bet that cleaned up the town!"

Mary Rose grasped the computer as if someone might tear it away from her. "Oh, and I loved Princess Di," she said. "Here's a headline about her. *Diana was alive just hours before her death.*" Mary Rose giggled and then shot a fleeting, worried look at Hadley who was smiling along with the others.

It was the giggles that attracted Wiley and Alphonso, who were headed toward the little bistro near the dining room which contained a soft-serve ice cream machine and an afternoon treat. They detoured toward table 12. Without even a greeting, Wiley leaned over the computer. "Hey, Greatwood, get a load of this one, *Woman in sumo wrestling suit attacks ex-girlfriend in Gay Bar after waving to man dressed as a Snickers Bar.'* Why do you and I miss all the fun?"

Alphonso drove his scooter up to the table and Mary Rose moved the computer closer to him. He looked, waited a minute, then started to laugh. "Here's my kind of justice. *'Man who kills his lawyer gets new attorney.'* Let's make our own headline. How about, *'Ice cream big hit in retirement community, proving how easily old people are amused.'"*

They chuckled, stood up, pushed their chairs to the table and followed him into the Meadow Lakes Bistro where the ice cream machine stood waiting without a headline in sight. The sun shone into the dining room, even brighter than before.

And as they walked down the hall, every one of them, except Alphonso, stole a quick glance at Hadley.

Hadley Joy Morris-Whitfield was tall and stately with Vidal Sassoon hair that hung gracefully just below her ears and moved of its own accord when she turned her head. She had been a socialite and professional volunteer before her husband crashed and died in his private plane. He had been a big man who liked big cars and big dogs and while he wasn't always the most faithful, he adored Hadley and treated her like the trophy wives some of his colleagues had found to replace their wives who were getting older.

They had a good marriage with a lot of understanding and after he died, Hadley rattled around in her big McMansion in west Omaha and moved in short order to Meadow Lakes. At one time she lived in the biggest apartment in the building, but now she was comfortable in a spacious two bedroom big enough for the girls to still have movie marathons where a part of the fun was drinking cheap champagne and eating popcorn with goldfish crackers and M&Ms.

And her friends were watching her. They wanted to be there for her if she needed them. So far, when she did need help, she asked for it.

Before the snow had started to melt for the first time in months and the great snow mountains in parking lots began to turn to slush, Hadley had made a phone call. Like all of us, she had made phone calls that changed her life. This was one of those.

Earlier that autumn, they had been at Salem's Crossing, in the bed and breakfast Robbie thought she had inherited, when Hadley had a nightmare that Wes Longbow, her long-distant companion, had walked up a ramp onto the big front porch and suddenly disappeared.

She knew in her dream he had died.

Days later, as the handsome Indian sheriff was getting ready to board a plane to return to his cabin on the West Coast, he suffered a severe heart attack. He had survived, gotten a little stronger and mostly because of a horrendous winter, had stayed in

Hadley's apartment until just a month or so ago.

After he had gotten home,as agreed, Hadley called him every day.

Then, one day, he didn't answer.

Borrowing a detective technique from Marge Aaron, Hadley had taken Wes's cell phone while he was napping in her big chair. She had found the phone number of his best friend, Phillip White Feather, another Native American who checked Wes's cabin while he was gone. She had put Phil's number in her phone. Just in case.

When Wes didn't answer that afternoon, she called Phil. He promised to go at once to his friend's cabin and check. Hadley had paced in her apartment waiting for him to call back. She had paced down the hall to the dining room and back. She had walked back down her corridor and climbed the stairs to the floor above. She had looked at her watch every two minutes. She had prayed and struggled to keep from crying. She had clenched her fists until her knuckles were white.

She had waited just like this for word from the air control center when her husband's plane had gone missing and she hated it. She hated not being able to stop imagining the worst, not being able to stop worrying, no matter what she told herself. She hated being so helpless.

Then her phone rang just as she reached the landing between floors. The call had come. Phil White Feather's number appeared green on her phone screen. Her hands were cold as she answered. She could feel her heart stomping inside her chest and her hands shook – just a little. She had always been the calm, collected one during a crisis and she was no different now.

"Hello Phil," she whispered into the phone. The man on the other end took a deep breath.

"It's not good news, Hadley. I found Wes. He was in his recliner, head turned to watch the sunset. Looks like he passed away last evening. He's been gone for a few hours."

There was a pause.

"Thanks, Phil. It's not unexpected but that doesn't make it easier." She smiled a sad smile. She had always wondered about using words like "passed away." Was it like passing a grade in school? Was there a place called "Away" that you went past? And "gone" had always interested her. That was more accurate. The spirit that had been Wes Longbow, retired sheriff, wasn't here anymore.

Phil's voice came back on the phone. "He had all his arrangements made to go back to the tribe and be buried there with only the tribal elders present." Phil paused again. "I'm sorry about that, Hadley. You know how private he was and he wouldn't want you to grieve."

Hadley smiled. Like she could help it, not grieving, that is. White Feather wasn't finished. "He left a box here for you. It's ready to be shipped. I'll see that it goes out right away." There was a second or two of silence. "You okay?"

"I'm okay, Phil. We had a great relationship and I was lucky to know him. I have only good memories and unfortunately, this is just part of life. At our age we lose a lot of people. Thanks for checking on him. Thanks for taking care of him."

She pressed the "END" button on her phone and sat down on the top step leading down to her floor. She sat there for a good five minutes, then she stood up and walked slowly down the stairs toward her apartment, holding tight to the handrail.

Scenes from *Gone with the Wind* flashed through her memory and Scarlett O'Hara's words rang out in her mind. "I'll think about it tomorrow. I can stand it then. Tomorrow is another day." But as Hadley Joy Morris-Whitfield's foot reached the end of the stairs, she knew she would think about it every day, maybe even for the rest of her life.

As soon as Hadley closed the stairway door behind her, she clicked on the text icon on her phone. "Bistro. Now," she typed in and hit SEND. The message darted through the big building and lit up the phones of Marge Aaron, Robinson Leary and Mary Rose McGill. Immediately they left their apartments and arrived at Meadow Lakes' friendly little Bistro just seconds after Hadley took a chair at one of the ice cream tables. They pulled up chairs around her, all of them looking serious and intent.

Hadley didn't mince words. "Wes Longbow is dead." She looked into the face of each of her friends. "Phillip White Feather found him just minutes ago. He died watching the sunset last night. He's to be buried by his tribe, no one else is invited and that's kind of it. I will be sad for a while of course, but I have wonderful memories that will always be some of the highlights of my life, so I don't want you fussing or worrying about me."

That was the first time they looked at her. She was stoic. Then three pairs of hands reached for hers. No one spoke.

Finally Hadley broke the silence, "All of you know I'm not much of a public crier. I tend to have

DTTs, Designated Tear Times, alone and when it's comfortable for me. I'll be fine. I can either see this as a time of my life that is a new adventure or I can be devastated. I don't devastate easily." She leaned forward on the table and smiled at them. "I also have STDs. Strength, Determination, Tenderness and Smarts. I don't have all that many years left myself and I don't want to miss anything. I have a good son here in town and good grandchildren. I have you three and the other friends here. I have all the support I need and mine is not a personality to be down or depressed a lot.

"For right now, what I want to do is get out of here. We've been locked in all this winter of our discontent. I want to put on our coats and head for Ted and Wally's and a double dip of ice cream." She looked at Marge. "If you want to text Wiley and Alphonso to meet us there, that would be nice." She stood up. Marge reached for her cell phone and hit her own text icon. Without a word, they turned and headed toward their apartments to get their coats. The best ice cream parlor in Omaha was waiting for them in the Old Market with hundreds of flavors written on the wall, waiting to be chosen as the comfort food of choice.

The Box arrived just four days after Hadley had heard the news. It was large and cumbersome and when Sheryl called from the office to tell her a package was waiting for her, she added that Alphonso would deliver it on his scooter. He was at the door in five minutes.

"Thanks, Alphonso," Hadley said hefting the box off the scooter and onto the floor.

"Want me to stick around?" Alphonso asked.

"Nope. I want to do this alone." She kissed the top of his head as he backed out the door and immediately walked across her kitchen to get a knife from her knife rack to cut open the box. Thick brown packing paper was folded over the top to protect whatever was inside. She threw it off onto the floor and began to lift out wrapped objects and smaller boxes. She could see that the bottom half of the box was lined with Wes's favorite Navajo rug, exquisitely woven in colors of the sunset he had watched on his last day on earth.

She lifted out a plastic zip-lock bag and slid out five men's rings and a small ring box. There was a note that slid out with them. "Had – I've enjoyed these rings. Have them resized to fit your fingers. The one in the box belonged to my mother."

The rings were all silver and turquoise. "Very Indian," she thought and she smiled. They were beautiful. She opened the little box. The ring inside was obviously his mother's wedding band, inlaid with red and blue turquoise, it shown, its silver gleaming, its colors brilliant. "He had it cleaned for me," she thought. Wes had known for a long time he was dying. He had taken care of things.

A clear plastic box held five beautiful eagle feathers. Another box held the most beautiful Navajo necklace she had ever seen, a squash blossom white opal with red and blue turquoise set within it. A pair of matching earrings was wrapped in tissue paper in the bottom of the box, more memories of his mother.

The object that brought tears to her eyes was in another box. There was a framed photo of Hadley and Wes, taken at a market when she had visited him a few years before. Along with it was a large, well-worn dog collar, still holding the soft, warm, comfortable smell of a good dog. The good dog had been in the picture with them. Apache was a Bernese Mountain Dog, big, black with white and rust markings and the most beautiful eyes Hadley had ever seen on a dog. She sat on the floor holding the collar and weeping. The big dog had died the year before Wes, and as she thought about it, she realized it had been exactly a year to the day. Had Apache come for him? Had he gone home with the big dog running by his side? She hoped so. She put her head in her hands and sobbed.

As she sorted the gifts, she thought how often we get presents and sometimes we get true gifts. These were gifts. The tears in her eyes almost caused her to miss a sheet of paper that had fallen out of the box. She opened it, adjusted her glasses and read:

For Hadley
You have brightened my days
Made the sun shine
Made the rain gentle
Made me laugh
Made me listen better
And made me mind my manners in restaurants.
In many ways you made me who I am in my old age:
A man who learned how to love
before it was too late.
I thank you.
Philamaymaye

She knew the last word had to be Indian for "Thank You."

She held the simple little poem to her heart and whispered three words, "Thank you, too." She picked things up and put the dog collar and picture on a shelf in her bedroom. She thought how precious a cheap dog collar and old photo could be. She wished she had a big, good dog to hug right then.

Geoffrey was such a dog, big and good with an unusual dose of stupid to his credit. An oversized dark mastiff, Geoffrey had come to Meadow Lakes as the security officer for the wicked Thorny Busch. He had scared Mary Rose out of her wits and finally cornered her on a couch. He jumped on her and threw couch, woman and dog to the floor and avidly licked off her makeup while his tail beat out a marching band beat on the overturned couch. From that moment on, he had been her dog.

Geoffrey loved Mary Rose. He lived for treats and rides in the Hummer where he could put his head out the window and let the wind blow back his big black ears. He was awkward without a trace of grace in his long, oversized legs. He looked like a Great Dane who didn't make the cut. He was loving and charming and sweet and a total, unabashed coward. Geoffrey turned out to be afraid of everything except makeup. He made Scooby Doo look like a holy terror.

Part Two

Road Trips and Reunions

Marge: "Mary Rose you're talking to yourself again."
Mary Rose: "I know. I like having a conversation
with an intelligent person."

Robbie: "It is so hard getting old!
Everything either dries up or leaks."
Hadley: "Or shifts like bad sand.
Remember Cross Your Heart Bras?
Now they're Cross Your Waist Bras."

Mary Rose: "I was doing my Bible lesson
and did you know God promised
that good and obedient wives
would be found in all corners of the earth?"
Robbie: "Then God made the earth round
and laughed and laughed."

Marge: "I have legs by Rand McNally with more
red and blue lines than a scaled map of Nebraska."
Hadley: "I have a question. How much
Healthy Choice ice cream
can I eat before it stops being a healthy choice?"

If winter in Omaha was harsh, spring and summer came in like a locomotive on a downhill track. The trees burst into bloom as if relieved the snow had melted. One day Hadley opened her window to hear an explosion of honking geese and ducks. "There will be snow and there will be rain," she said to the V of waterfowl she was watching fly over the roof of Meadow Lakes, "but there will come a day when the birds fly north again."

The girls spent time in the Old Market, had long lunches at Marks Bistro, their favorite restaurant, and walked across the pedestrian bridge that overlooked small boats and big barges making their way up and down the Missouri River. They walked slower than they had the first time they crossed it years ago, and when they were in the Old Market, they stopped more frequently.

One day, they climbed in the Hummer and took Geoffrey to the dog park. Mary Rose opened the gate and he bounded in, sniffed for exactly thirty seconds and lay down, looking up at them with a big grin. Mary Rose went through the gate and tried to get him to stand up and exercise. He licked her face and rolled over to have his belly rubbed, an even bigger grin covering his massive square face. Hadley threw his ball. He got up, stretched, yawned and expelled a scented cloud of gas, then trotted over to the ball. He picked it up in his teeth, looked at them and lay back down. Finally Mary Rose yelled, "Geoffrey! Ride!" and he dashed through the gate and stood by the Hummer. "Maybe the dog park was designed for humans," Mary Rose concluded.

Her daughters and granddaughters had come for Mother's Day. Hadley's son and his new lady had brought his children and a couple of their friends. Even Marge's children from Chicago and Washington,D.C., arrived for the holiday weekend. They all got along well and they all had a good time. The girls were delighted to see them, enjoyed showing them off and were worn out and relieved when they left.

"There were so many young people here," Robbie said, "For *them* Meadow Lakes must be like visiting a fossil bed." Robbie was the only one with no children.

Hadley had her ups and downs, but so did everyone else in the retirement community. The older you get, the more people you lose to death. They ate their meals together and had a day-long Sean Connery movie marathon in Hadley's apartment, pigging down on popcorn filled with goldfish crackers and M&Ms and drinking cheap champagne. They played poker with Wiley now and then and piled into Alphonso's van to go to a Pops Concert at the Holland Center in downtown Omaha.

Then, just as the last blossom of spring dropped listlessly to the ground, the hot winds of summer began to sweep across the northern plains. Another season had arrived, this one riding high on a strong wind from the south.

Marge was reading from the Omaha World Herald one morning while they were extending breakfast into mid-morning coffee. Wiley was seated with them, arguing over an editorial Marge had just read, when Alphonso wheeled up with a letter for Robbie. "Mailman just came and this looked important," he said. It was a fancy envelope with a gold embossed return address: *S. McKooter, Bed and Breakfast, Salem's Crossing, Nebraska.*

"Oh great," Robbie sighed. "It's from Scooter." She ripped open the envelope and took out a sheet of paper with three little words written on it.

Call me now!

"She never took down my phone number," Robbie said.

"She's computer savvy," Hadley added. "She could have googled you."

Marge added her two cents worth. "She could have called 411 and gotten your number on her cell phone." Wiley laughed, "All those ideas would have taken away the drama. Call her, Rob."

Robinson Leary picked up her phone. "We may regret this," she said, a frown slowly creasing her forehead.

A Nice Little Reunion

"What do you mean you need our help, Scooter? And where the heck are you? It sounds like it's raining." Robbie looked at her three friends, shook her head, shrugged her shoulders and rolled her eyes.

"It IS raining!" Scooter McKooter's voice came over Robbie's speaker phone. "But I needed a cigarette so I'm out here getting wet."

"How can you smoke a wet cigarette?" Marge asked loudly.

"I put a condom over it," Scooter shouted back, equally loud. "You should have seen the pharmacist when I told him this well-over-eighty-year-old lady wanted a box of condoms. He finally asked me what brand and I told him I didn't care as long as it fit a Camel." She cackled like the wicked witch of the west.

Scooter McKooter had tricked the girls into coming to her "haunted" bed and breakfast in Salem's Crossing, Nebraska, about one hundred miles west of Omaha on the Loup River. She had frightened them, worried them and eventually shown herself and accepted their reluctant friendship and help. Now Scooter needed help again.

"There's this new girl, Brenda Lee Colton, who has inherited the fishing resort upriver at Scenic Pont. She's going to put me out of business when the big reunion comes. She has a little motel and cabins and she's a good cook, too."

"Reunion?" all four girls said together.

"The Great Puritan Descendants Reunion," Scooter replied. "It's the first week of July and everyone whose Puritan ancestors were here will be coming back to celebrate, get together, renew old friendships, and have a good time. It's a crazy time and it only comes every ten years. It's wonderful, delightful, where everyone wants to be."

The girls looked at each other. "Frankly, Scooter, you're making it sound too good to be true," Robbie said.

Scooter's voice changed. "Ok, it sucks, but the B and B will be full and I need help cooking and cleaning and entertaining." Her voice took on a practiced whine. "You young women all know I'm too old to do it all by myself." A sniff. A sigh.

"What do you think, *young women*?" Robbie asked her friends. Marge made a face where she sneered, grimaced and pulled at a grey curl.

Mary Rose McGill stood up, leaned one hand on the table and raised the other one to get ready for high fives. "Road Trip!" she yelled. The other three slapped her hand.

"When do you want us, Scooter?"

"As soon as you can get your fat fannies here. You can hook the trailer up to the electric, sewer and water beside the house. There sure as hell isn't room inside for all you women."

"Ah!" Robbie said. "The real Scooter McKooter has returned. We can probably leave day after tomorrow." She hit the END CALL button. "Why do I think of the Maxine character on the greeting cards every time I think of Scooter?"

"A Puritan Reunion," Hadley grinned. "I bet when they all look at each other what they see becomes a very effective form of birth control."

Marge laughed. "You know the most effective form of birth control over age fifty?" They leaned toward her. "Nudity," she whispered.

Mary Rose grinned. "I know a religious Puritan joke." She took a deep breath. "This Puritan was going to church and all at once Satan appeared in front of him. The Puritan looked at him and shrugged, then walked past him. Satan yelled at him. 'Do you not know who I am?"

The man said, 'Yep, sure do.'

Satan said, 'Aren't you afraid of me?'

The man shook his head. 'Nope, sure ain't.'

Satan was a little perturbed, so he said. 'Why aren't you afraid of me?'

The man just looked at him, 'Been married to your sister for 31 years.'

Willie Nelson was wailing their traveling music and they were singing along to "On the Road Again" as the Hummer and trailer moved across Nebraska. The Hummer was the biggest made and pulled the long travel trailer as if it wasn't there.

Geoffrey slept in the far back, one paw covering his ear to keep out the singing. The corn was up and growing and soon would be high as an elephant's eye for sure. The Platte River, lifeline for the pioneers in their wagon trains west, ran full after a recent rain. In spring and fall it became the second largest wildfowl migration site in the world, hosting nearly a million ducks, geese, sandhill and whooping cranes, among other birds.

Willie's CD ended and they rode a while in silence for a short while. Suddenly, Mary Rose jumped. "Oh, no! Does Scooter have cable?"

"I don't remember even seeing a TV," Marge said from the driver's seat.

"I forgot to record *The Walking Dead.* Dang!"

Hadley looked at her, seated by the other window in the back seat. "Mary Rose McGill! How can you watch that show?"

"Hey!" Mary Rose looked back at her. "Just remember, girlfriend, if there's a Zombie apocalypse and they want to turn us into human happy meals, I'm the only one here who knows how to kill a Zombie."

"And how do you do that?" Robbie asked from the front passenger seat.

"You have to have a sword and a whole lot of kitchen utensils."

No one knew what else to say, then Mary Rose added, "This is season five and the lawns in the show are always mowed. A world of zombies and one of them must have a rotary mower."

Marge punched in Willie Nelson again. Geoffrey opened one eye then returned the paw that had slipped down off his ear. Nebraska rolled by under their wheels.

Dolls for Big Girls

The huge Victorian mansion with its high-roofed three stories and double turrets loomed beautifully in the late afternoon sun. The trees around it were in full leaf and shaded the big lawn. Scooter had painted it in Queen Anne mansion pastels and a simple new sign hung above the gate, saying only *Bed and Breakfast.* They climbed out of the Hummer and stretched. Geoffrey found a tree then followed them inside.

The last time they had walked in the door, cobwebs and mice had greeted them. The massive fireplace in the dining room had revolved to scare them with a mummy, the moose head on the opposite wall leered at them and a panel rolled back from each eye so anyone who could stick their head in far enough could watch them.

Now, instead of dust and rodent urine, the smell was of good candles and furniture polish. A front table had become a registration desk for guests and the chandelier above it was sparkling and clean. The entire mansion was welcoming and inviting and spotless throughout. Also clean was the woman sitting in one of the big wing back chairs in front of the fireplace. The woman in the other chair was questionable.

Scooter McKooter was covered with dust but Geoffrey didn't care. He bounded across the entry hall, put his big head in her lap, looked up with his puppy-dog eyes and drooled on to her skirt. She scratched his ears. A minute later, he was begging Mary Rose to let him outside. She opened the door and he leaped off the porch after an imaginary victim.

There were cobwebs in Scooter's hair and the dirty smock she wore over her long gray skirt was stained and ragged. Her hair, dyed a dismal red, was in spikes like Phyllis Diller's. There were dirt streaks on her face and her nails were broken and grimy. She grinned a lopsided grin. "Basement's finally cleaned. Just finished. Got two more beds set up down there and it looks real cozy."

Scooter was Doctor McKooter and had worked at Creighton University with the other PhD in the room, Robinson Leary. She was short, stooped and when she walked, due to her stooped shoulders, she swung one arm in front of her. She called it her Ape Walk. She didn't get up, but the other woman stood.

She was trim and attractive with brown hair and wearing jeans and a tee shirt that had "Scenic Point Resort" on the front. Her sneakers were white and clean. She wasn't wearing socks. "Brenda Lee Colton," she said, holding out her hand. "I'm the competition." They all shook hands.

As she let go of Brenda Lee's hand, Hadley looked just beyond her and her eyes got wide. "Look, girls." She pointed to a round table in the middle of the entrance to the long dining room. The top of the table was covered with a circular mirror and on it sat ten beautiful statues or dolls, whichever fit the viewer's fancy. About a foot high and beautifully carved with happy-looking porcelain faces, their clothes were made of expensive cloth and seemed to accurately represent Puritan fashion. There were six little men and four doll-like women. In the center was a carved lamppost surrounded by tiny evergreen bushes. The four girls went to the table and each picked up one of the statue-dolls.

"They're sweet," Robbie said. "And look at this, girls." She picked up a black frame with a piece of soft pink computer paper inside. "It's a take-off on the old Agatha Christie poem, 'Ten Little Soldier Boys,' only this is 'Ten Little Puritans' and different. Hope we aren't trapped in the same murderous story." She passed the framed poem around. No one paid much attention. They were all attracted to the statues that were like dolls for grownup girls. Scooter and Brenda paid no attention either.

Marge turned her statue of a woman upside down. "They're wearing little tiny underwear."

"But none of the ladies are dressed in black," Mary Rose observed. "I thought Puritans always wore black." It was true. The little female statues had dresses of every color of the rainbow. The only commonalities were their black shoes, white aprons and white bonnets.

Robbie spoke up, holding one of the little men in her hand. "Black dye was expensive. Usually only clergy and high officials could wear black."

Mary Rose looked at Hadley. "How does she always know that stuff?"

The six male statues all had black hats with gold buckles and different colored hat bands. Their suits were fitted at the waist with trousers that were tied just below the knees. White stockings ended in black shoes, also adorned with buckles.

"Ten Little Puritans," Hadley said, putting her doll down and looking at Robbie.

"As I said, just like in Agatha Christie's mystery," Robbie muttered. "The title was *Then There Were None*, but what everyone remembers is the poem. 'Ten little soldier boys went out to dine – one went and choked himself and then there were nine.' Everyone in her story died." There was a silence.

Loudly, Hadley said, "Scooter, where did you get these little Puritan dolls? They must be worth well over one hundred dollars each. We're looking at more than a thousand dollars of Puritanism here." But their host neither heard nor responded. They all turned toward Scooter and Brenda.

Both women were standing. Brenda was a head taller than Scooter and was bending down to be nose-to-nose with her.

"I'm wiping you out, girlfriend," Scooter said.

"We can work together or I can bury you," Brenda said, and she squared her shoulders, nodded to the girls and the dolls and walked out the door.

"Ooooooh kay" Marge said, looking at Scooter. "What was that all about?"

"She's a braggart and arrogant. I don't like her," Scooter sniffed, breathed in some of her own dust and sneezed loudly.

Robbie looked around, "Let's go hook up the trailer." They all turned and went back outside where Geoffrey was waiting for them, happily holding a long-dead squirrel in his teeth.

The Outhouse

"Holy Moly," Robbie said. "Look at what she's done!" Their eyes followed to where her finger was pointing. Marge had backed the trailer up close to the side of the big house. It had only taken her two tries, three cuss words and frantic waving and gesturing from Hadley to get it perfect.

Scooter had arranged for two spaces for campers, both with sewer lines leading into the mansion's waste system. There were electric and water outlets and all the comforts of a regular campground. Now they were all looking behind the house to where Robinson Leary was pointing and smiling. There, sitting tall and proud was a genuine, old fashioned outhouse.

"It's pink!" Mary Rose exclaimed.

"It has the half-moon in the door," Hadley said.

Marge grinned. "Grandchildren today have no idea what a real outhouse is and that's a real outhouse."

Robbie put her hands on her hips, "Kids today have tasteless porta potties. I'm betting you this is a two-holer." She moved toward the outhouse and began to laugh. "My grandmother didn't have electricity or running water. She said she had 'three rooms and a path' instead of a 'bath'". Geoffrey was sniffing and wagging his way around the little structure.

They walked to the outhouse, which was obviously an original, recently moved to this location and sporting a new coat of bright pink paint. The brass hinges creaked when Marge opened the door. They crowded around to look inside and Robbie and Hadley stepped in to make room for them to see.

"Yep," Hadley said, "two-holer."

"Look at the signs," Mary Rose giggled.

Covering the entire wall above the two toilet holes were framed signs on papers of various colors. Marge read the first one which was about three feet above the hole on the right. "If you can pee this high the fire department wants you." She went on. "These are my kind of signs; listen to this one, 'Police toilet stolen. Cops have nothing to go on.'"

Robbie took up the challenge with the next sign, "No drugs or nuclear weapons allowed in this outhouse." Mary Rose shook her head. "That is so Scooter. I like this one: 'Those with shorter bats please stand closer to home plate.'" She giggled again.

"My turn," Hadley said, when she started to laugh out loud at a metal sign hung in the exact middle of the wall.

"My aim is to keep this bathroom clean.

Gentlemen, your careful aim will be appreciated.

Please stand closer.
Your weapon is shorter than you think.

Ladies, please remain seated for the entire
performance."

Marge smiled and read. "Never drop cigarettes down
these holes. Remember, gas can explode."

The side walls each held at least ten toilet paper
holders filled with rolls of various kinds of toilet
tissue. A simple sign graced each wall, "Choose
carefully, wiping is an art form." Delicate braided
rugs lay in front of each hole.

Propped carefully in one corner was a genuine Sears
and Roebuck Catalog, the kind that used to be used
for toilet paper. It was carefully encased in a plastic
box frame. Not encased was a neat stack of corn cobs
in the opposite corner, also used for toilet paper in
the old days. *The Bathroom Book of Jokes* lay between
the holes and a framed picture of a baby boy on a
potty hung above the book. "Effort!" was written
under the picture.

"This is a masterpiece," Hadley said, pulling out her phone and snapping a picture.

"And a good idea," Robbie said. "It's obviously for *overflow* when the B&B is full." She pushed against the wall. "No one is going to push this sucker over. My aunt and uncle were making out in an outhouse when they were teenagers and his buddies pushed it over. They ended up in a ditch smelling to high heaven. Her father had to help them out and her blouse was unbuttoned."

Marge and Hadley did eye rolls. Mary Rose grinned from ear to ear. "Everybody out," she said. "While I'm here, I might as well pee."

Ten Real Puritans

Ken David David, a Goth wannabe and best friend to Geoffrey, bounded in the door along with the happy mastiff first thing the next morning. The dog had obviously been taken for a run by Ken David before they made an appearance. His doggie eyes were bright, he was prancing beside the young man and his tongue was hanging out. The girls were helping Scooter set up an extra table to register the Puritan descendants due to arrive that morning. They dropped what they were doing and went forward to hug Ken David, whose last name really was David.

They had met the young Goth when he pretended to rob the Salem's Crossing Bank and they refused to lie down on the floor, even though he had a rifle in his hands. Marge had tasered him in the balls and then adopted him as a surrogate grandson of all four women. He was here to help carry luggage and be, as Scooter put it, "the one with the strong back and weak mind." It fit.

Just as the last old-fashioned fountain pen was positioned beside the antique reproduction guest registers Scooter had ordered online, and just as Ken David took the last bite of the donut he had swiped from the Old Country Roses serving plate on one of the tables, the first car pulled up into the circle drive in front of the bed and breakfast. An attractive couple in their fifties got out, took an approving look at the mansion and began to walk up the path leading to the porch. All five women and Ken David each took a deep breath. Geoffrey quietly took his own donut off the plate while his people were all looking outside.

"Hello and welcome," Scooter said, opening the door for her first guests.

Everyone smiled, nodded and Hadley and Marge both sat down at the tables, waiting to see which the couple would choose. The sound of a second car echoed in from the driveway. Guests were arriving.

"We're the Simptums," the lady said. She was dressed in an attractive jogging suit which subtly said she had money. Her husband was in jeans, sneakers and a crewneck shirt.

"The Simptums," Hadley said, urging them to come toward her table.

"Ella and Sam," the woman replied. Hadley began to write.

"Oh for Pete's sake," Robbie whispered and she walked over and bent down close to Marge's ear. "Reverse the first names."

Marge thought for a second then grinned. "Sam and Ella Simptums," Marge whispered back, so softly Robbie could barely hear her. "Salmonella Symptoms. We'll hope they're not poison people." Scooter was scowling at them. They looked up and gave her an innocent, "Who me?" look. Hadley gave the Simptums their room key, Ken David hoisted the luggage in both arms and headed for a door in the nearest turret.

Next to arrive were two elderly gentlemen dressed in plaid shorts, white tee shirts and sandals over black socks. Both had straw hats which they removed as soon as they entered. One headed toward Marge, the other toward Hadley.

"Good morning," Marge said.

"Hello, Sweetheart. We have a room reserved with two beds. We're the Bahl brothers."

Marge picked up her pen, ready to write, and smiled at the man who must be in his nineties.

"I'm Harry Bahls. My brother over there is Buster."

Robbie did an eye roll. Mary Rose was holding a plate of donuts and Robbie had just gotten a tray of juice glasses filled with orange juice from the kitchen. Each guest was to have juice and a donut. Two coffee urns graced the sideboard along with glass cups waiting to be filled and enjoyed. The Simptums had gulped their juice down on the way to the stairs, filled two coffee cups and passed on the donuts, Robbie looked at the donut plate and felt relieved. She could tell two were missing and Ken David and Geoffrey both had donut crumbs on their lips.

"What were their names again?" Robbie asked Mary Rose in another whisper.

"The Bahls, Harry and Buster."

"Harry Bahls and Buster Bahls," Robbie did another eye roll and shook her head. "Where do these names come from? And it isn't even 10am!"

Mary Rose smiled and batted her eyelashes. "I think they're sweet. Maybe one of them is married to a lady named Rosie Bahls. That would be cheery." Robbie sighed and offered the Bahl brothers donuts and juice.

"I'm ninety-two years old," Harry Bahls said. "Some people want to turn their odometers back, but not me. I want people to know how old I am. I've been on a lot of roads in my life and some of them weren't paved. Let me know if you want to party, girlie." He smiled, winked and actually gave Robbie a quick pat on the fanny.

His brother smiled at him then he winked at Robbie, too. "He spent a fortune on deodorant then discovered he didn't need it since people didn't get close to him because they didn't like him." He tossed his room key to Ken David who headed toward their car to collect their luggage. The two old gentlemen headed back for the porch and two of the rockers waiting to be enjoyed. They settled in and began to munch on their donuts and sip their juice.

Two genuine Puritan descendants were next, sisters who were so old they looked as if they belonged with the Bahls. Abstinence Evermore and Patience Evenow made sure everyone in the room knew there were streets named after their great grandmothers. The two ladies were beautiful with pure white hair and both wore bright print dresses and white sneakers. Abstinence carried a large summer hat which she gracefully kept at her side. They went after donuts, coffee and juice as if they hadn't eaten all week.

After a couple named Ophelia and Royal Payne arrived, not speaking to each other and dressed like twins, Robbie went into the kitchen, crossed her arms on the counter by the sink and laughed until tears dripped onto the countertop.

Ophelia was plump, walked with a cane and had stringy hair that was turning a mousey grey. Royal, a snooty businessman who sold caskets reminded Hadley of a mean John Candy in the *Planes, Trains and Automobiles* movie. Only she was pretty sure John Candy was never mean. Royal looked as if he could pleasantly murder his wife or anyone else who got in his way. Ophelia spent a moment admiring Marge's red cane and Marge, while appreciative, would never tell her what those "pretty pieces of bling" did when pushed.

The full house was rounded out by two gentlemen in their mid-fifties wearing khakis, polo shirts and sandals with no socks. Remember Knott said he was a banker and his partner, DieWell Barebones was a lawyer. They were both handsome and relaxed and instantly likeable. DieWell told Mary Rose that his name was genuine Puritan and the Barebones family had the best and strangest names in the history of Puritanism.

The guests were all here. Marge read the names as soon as Ken David David disappeared with the last piece of luggage:

Sam and Ella Simptums

Harry Bahls and Buster Bahls

Ophelia and Royal Payne

Abstinence Evermore and Patience Evenow

Remember Knott and DieWell Barebones

"Six men and four women," Hadley said.

"Just like the little dolls," Marge added.

Robbie looked at Mary Rose. They both looked a little worried. Geoffrey, who had been sitting up behaving himself while the guest checked in, leaned on Mary Rose and looked for a hug. He got one and no one could tell whether he or the mistress he loved needed it more.

The girls began to clean up.

A Red –Tailed Hawk

Hadley took the empty Old Country Roses donut
plate to the kitchen and walked back into the foyer
to help take down the registration tables. Just as
her hand reached out to collapse the first one, she
looked out the front door with the beautiful oval of
beveled glass secure in the center. Through the glass
she could see a red-tailed hawk circling in the field
across the road. She dropped her hand from the table
and walked to the porch. The Bahl brothers were
nowhere to be seen, probably in their room, but the
hawk was swooping and gliding with more grace
than Hadley could imagine. Suddenly, it dived toward
the ground and came up with a long snake in its
beak. Without giving her a look, it careened over the
treetops and out of sight, as glorious in its departure
as anything in nature could be.

Hadley sighed and looked at the ramp coming up the
porch. Last year Wiley Vondra, Alphonso Greatwood
and Wes Longbow had built the handicap ramp for
Alphonso's scooter. After Hadley's frightening dream
where Wes walked up the ramp and disappeared and
she knew it meant he would die, she had watched
the three men finish the ramp. When Wes started
to walk up it, she hurried to his side and led him
around to the steps. She took him inside, told him her
dream and listened to him laugh, then felt his hug.
Now Wes Longbow was indeed dead. He had walked

up the ramp to wherever we go after we die and she would never see, touch or feel him again. She would never hear that laugh or look at that craggy Native American face. Hadley looked at the trees where the hawk had flown and realized her cheeks were wet with tears.

Ten little Puritans dressed up so fine,
One walked on water and then there were nine.

Scooter had offered her guests optional meals, so while some had gone off to town to meet old friends and see what had changed; most had remained for a build-your-own-sandwich buffet the girls had set up on the big dining room table. The mounted moose head surveyed the scene and Mary Rose mentioned to Marge that they should all take turns sometime crawling into the head and spying on the guests through the eye of the moose. A panel slid back in each eye and a human could watch out over the dining room. Marge had agreed.

As Robbie set the plates down on the table, a monstrous clap of thunder reverberated throughout the house and rain pounded against the windows.

"Oh My God," Harry Bahls exclaimed. "My car windows are down."

Mary Rose smiled at him. "Don't worry Mr. Bahls, it's a fake storm. Scooter can pull a lever in the attic and a storm rages, but it's really only on the inside."

She didn't notice that Geoffrey had taken refuge under the table rapidly swallowing a slice of ham while he hid from the thunder.

Harry Bahls paid no attention. With a slight limp and holding his straw hat to his head, he bounded, as fast as a ninety-two year old can bound, out the front door just as lightning flashed and thunder roared again. The rest of the guests shivered, some hugged themselves and looked anxiously out the windows where rain was streaming down in currents.

"Storm or no storm," DieWell Barebones said, "I'm hungry!" and he grabbed a plate, stacked two slices of bread on it and made his way down the buffet toward various lunch meats, cheeses and fruit. The rest followed.

"Scooter's letting that storm go on for a long time," Marge said, looking up at Hadley. Hadley nodded and put the last bite of her sandwich in her mouth.

"Have you seen my brother?" Buster Bahls was standing directly behind them, looking curious.

"As a matter of fact," Marge answered, "not since he left to close his car windows."

The storm stopped just as Marge, Hadley and Buster hurried to the door. Marge opened it and looked out. "Well, I'll be. It was a real storm."

The sidewalk and circular drive were soaking wet. Water stood in puddles all around the parked cars, one of which belonged to Harry Bahls and the windows were still rolled partway down.

"He never got the windows up." Marge said.

"All that water's going to ruin his new sandals," Buster said, shaking his head. "He's going to be pissed."

"Look," Hadley said, pointing toward the road. In the distance they could see an Amish carriage, pulled by a black horse, turning the corner and heading toward town. Scooter stuck her head out the door just as Hadley pointed to the vanishing carriage.

"That would be Stonewell Stolzfoos. He's one of the Amish here and he raises horses. He's offering carriage rides to the reunion folks." She snorted. "Charges an arm and a leg and gets it, too. Stupid tourists."

Geoffrey came through the door and leaned against Hadley. He looked at the carriage, growled at the vanishing horse and sat, looking up expectantly.

Hadley absentmindedly rubbed his head.

Buster Bahls walked down the driveway to his brother's car and looked inside. "He's got to have really soaked his sandals," he called back to the little group on the porch.

"Maybe he's in the outhouse," Marge suggested, pointing to the back of the house. Buster went to look.

Inside, the plates were in the new dishwasher, the sandwiches were bagged and in the refrigerator and Scooter, Mary Rose and the remaining guests were seated in the big chairs in the parlor, talking as if they had known each other for years.

Robbie was coming through the dining room with her own cup of coffee. She glanced sideways as she headed toward the laughter coming from the parlor conversations, then, in a loud whisper said, "Hey, Girls!" Marge and Hadley looked at her where she had stopped by the round mirrored table holding the Puritan dolls. "Am I counting wrong?"

They moved toward her. Marge began to point at each doll and count, "One, two, three, four, five, six, seven, eight……..*NINE!* There's one missing." She bent down and looked under the table. "It didn't fall off."

Hadley looked around, "Geoffrey! Come here!"
The big dog appeared from the kitchen, more donut
crumbs on his lips. "Did you take a doll?" Geoffrey
wagged and put his wet lips on Hadley's hand, "I
think that's a 'no.'"

Nine little Puritans sure they would be late,
One hurried off and then there were eight.

"Oh, my!" Patience Evenow said, standing up from
her easy chair in the parlor. "We're going to be late
for the first icebreaker activity at the senior center.
Everyone coming back for the reunion will be there."
The rest of the guests stood with her and began
hurrying to their rooms to gather purses and any
other belongings they might need.

"Do you think Buster Bahls needs a ride?" Mary
Rose asked. "He's old and he didn't drive here, his
brother was behind the wheel. It would be nice to
at least ask him if we can help. Harry, too, if he has
shown up."

"Where is Buster?" Hadley asked.

"He was hurrying to the outhouse to see if Harry was
there last I knew," Marge said.

"I'll go look," Robbie volunteered. "It's still wet out
there and my shoes can take it."

Other guests poured out the door that Ken David David was politely holding open for them.

Marge's cell phone rang. Robbie's name showed up on caller ID. "Marge, Mr. Bahls is not out here anywhere. Can you check his room?"

Marge looked at Ken David David, "Ken David, did Buster Bahls go out the door with the others?" The young Goth shook his head and shrugged. "Will you be a dear and check his room for us?" Marge asked. Ken David sprinted up the stairs two at a time.

"I remember when I could do that," Hadley said, looking after him. In just a few seconds he appeared at the landing in front of the Bahl brothers room. "Nope," he said, shaking his head. "Not here."

Robbie came in through the kitchen door with Geoffrey at her side. "He's not anywhere on the property that I could see and of course brilliant dog here was only interested in trees and no help at all." The mastiff looked up at her with soft brown eyes and grinned.

"The Bahls probably got in a car with one of the other guests and we just didn't notice," Mary Rose said. "They were quite old but they seemed quite smart. They would find a way to town."

Robbie smiled and shook her head. "Smart? I read the other day where it was in 1874 that hockey teams started using those testicular guards, the cups. It wasn't until 1974 they started using helmets. It only took men one hundred years to realize they should probably also protect their brains." Geoffrey groaned and lay down at her feet. Robbie lifted one foot onto his back and moved it back and forth to rub his back.

Marge walked over to the mirrored table and pointed to the Puritan dolls. "Mary Rose, come count these, girl."

Mary Rose moved beside Marge and began to count the dolls. "One, two, three, four, five, six, seven..... EIGHT! You mean they've been disappearing along with our guests?"

Marge nodded. "And they're both men dolls missing just like our two missing old men. Something's going on here and I don't like it. I don't like it a bit! Scooter!"

Scooter McKooter shuffled in from the parlor.

"What?!"

"Fess up, woman. What's going on?"

Scooter looked confused. "What's going on is Stonewell the Amish is making a killing with that dumb horse and carriage! I just saw him round the corner on his second tour of the day. How can people be so dumb?"

They could tell by her look that she knew nothing about the missing men and dolls. "Scooter, where did you get the dolls?" Marge asked.

"I thought you sent them. They came last week by UPS."

"It wasn't us," Marge said. "Did you save the label?"

"Nope."

Ken David David came in through the door. "Just took a run; didn't see any Bahls at all."

It was past mid-afternoon. The B&B was clean, dishes put away and no one had signed up for dinner. They sat down in the chairs and settee facing the big fireplace and sighed. Just then, the door opened and Penstemon Primrose, the sweet old lady with dementia, walked in. Even though it was July in Nebraska, Penstemon wore a long black dress and ankle-high black boots. She walked past them toward her favorite bedroom, now belonging to the Simptums.

"Hello Stems," Scooter said. "I think it will be OK if you go up there. You'll be gone before our guests get back from town."

Penstemon smiled her soft smile. "Shut Up and Drink." And she disappeared into the bedroom.

Penstemon Primrose was cared for by the entire town. Every afternoon she came to Scooter's place and took a short nap, after which she went to the local tavern, Shut Up and Drink, to meet one of her three boyfriends, Jack Daniels, Johnny Walker or Jim Beam.

"That's a good idea," Robbie said. "Let's go to Shut Up and Drink and have a drink and pub grub. Maybe we'll see some Bahls there."

"That is almost funny," Marge said, grabbing her cane and struggling to her feet.

Mary Rose got up, then looked at the Puritan dolls and hesitated.

"Mary Rose?" Hadley asked.

"I had a thought," Mary Rose said, "but it got lonely and left."

Marge looked at her. "I understand. Sometimes things fall out of my brain while I sleep."

Geoffrey decided he wanted to be their lost thoughts. He bounded to the door, looked at his leash hanging on the coat rack and sat, blocking the door. Mary Rose hooked him up and they all headed for the Hummer, the town of Salem's Crossing and the Shut Up and Drink.

The little tavern was brimming with reunion goers. Laughter and music filled the air along with the combined smell of furniture polish and alcohol. Seated at a far table in one corner was a woman with her laptop open in front of her. She was concentrating with great intensity and reaching for her Stella beer in a tall, frosty glass. She picked it up without missing a beat on her keyboard, took a sip and set it down delicately.

"Touch of class, there," Hadley noted, noticing the beer.

"Oh, hello, hello!" Patience Evenow and Abstinence Evermore were seated alone at a table for six. "Come join us," Patience said, gesturing toward the empty chairs.

Humiliation Strykes, the dignified bartender came to their table wearing his apron, spotless white shirt and black bowtie. "Ladies, ladies! It's grand having you here. What can I get you?"

Patience was still holding her menu. "I need to study this, you all go ahead."

"Marge looked at the menu. "Let's do a bottle of chardonnay since there are six of us, and," she looked at the girls, "burgers all around?"

Everyone nodded except Patience. "Hummer, dear," she pointed to the menu. 'I can't have any grains or gluten, any dairy or sweets."

Robbie did an eye roll and Hadley leaned closer to hear. Hummer pointed to one of the salads. "That should be good," he suggested.

"Does it have garlic or onions?"

Hummer looked distressed and shook his head. "How about spices? Are there any on the salad at all?"

Hummer shook his head again.

"No salt, I hope." She batted her eyelashes at the bartender. "I don't want any dressing on that either, dear."

Marge leaned over to Hadley. "That leaves mustard," she whispered.

Hadley leaned back, "I used to have a sign that said, 'Eat Right. Exercise. Die Anyway.'"

"Five burgers and one plate of lettuce coming up," Hummer said, walking back toward the kitchen.

Abstinence smiled at them. "I understand you girls call yourselves the SOBs."

The girls looked confused. "SOBs?" Mary Rose asked. "What do you mean?"

"Spunky Old Broads," Abstinence said, her eyebrows having a conversation with her hairline. Patience shook her head and did an eye roll. "Actually, I think it might have been BOBs, Bitchy Old Broads,"

Mary Rose and Hadley laughed. "Close, but no cigar," Hadley said. "We're The BOOB Girls: The Burned Out Old Broads."

Robbie smiled. "I kind of like SOBs."

Abstinence patted Patience on the arm. "We can be the SOBs, dear."

They were quiet after their food came. The burgers were the old-fashioned kind the girls remembered from growing up, big, greasy, and tender with soft buns. They were melt-in-your-mouth with a high-calorie taste. There were no boxes or doggie bags for anyone except Patience, who took half her lettuce home and declared three times how healthy and delicious it was. The food police had invaded Salem's Crossing disguised as Puritans.

Just as they were finishing, Mary Rose asked for a bowl of water for Geoffrey who was tied at the end of the decorative old porch surrounding the front of the tavern. Hummer brought a large plastic bowl filled with cool water. Four ice cubes floated on top.

"Thanks, Hummer," Mary Rose smiled, getting up from her chair and walking slowly out the door so as to not splash any of the water in Geoffrey's bowl. In just minute, she opened the door, stuck her head in and motioned for the women at her table to come outside.

When they hurried through the door they saw Geoffrey, ignoring his water, braced on stiff legs, looking down the street in front of the tavern. Once again they saw the black horse and carriage belonging to Stonewell Stolzfoos rounding the corner two blocks away. A low, menacing growl was coming from the big dog's throat and he didn't turn toward his water until the carriage was totally out of sight.

"Gives me goosies," Mary Rose said, rubbing her arms. Marge nodded and took ahold of the red cane that always graced one arm. Hadley hugged herself and wished Wes Longbow was beside her; he would know what to do. Robbie shrugged and opened the door for them to go back inside.

They sat back down at the table with Patience and Abstinence to finish their drinks.

"I think we should check every place in town where we might find the Bahls," Marge said, holding her wine glass by its stem and turning it gently. She was staring into the last of the wine as if it held an answer.

"They're probably at the senior center," Patience guessed. "Abstinence and I grew up with them and if there are any women around, there will be Bahls."

"I can drink to that," Abstinence said, tipping her glass to her lips and getting the last drop out. She was a remarkably handsome woman, one who was ageless.

"If we don't find them, then what?" Mary Rose asked.

Marge looked at her. "We go see Matilda Minor-Milldew and bring the chief of police into the loop. She knows this town."

The writer at the corner table stood, stretched, finished the last of her beer and sat back down. She had never looked around or even seemed to be aware of her environment.

The six women at the table stood and, waving goodbye to Humiliation Strykes went out the door and to their separate cars. Geoffrey bounded into the Hummer before Mary Rose could get his water bowl back to the bartender inside.

The Search

Ophelia and Royal Payne were glaring at each other at a small table at the senior center. A man in a Puritan outfit, complete with hat two sizes too big, was reading something that dated back to the settlement of Salem's Crossing.

"You wonder what Puritans would want in the middle of the northern plains where the deer and the antelope really did roam," Mary Rose said.

They smiled and shook their heads. "Paynes are accounted for," Marge said. They piled into the Hummer and headed for the park, a square near the center of town. The Simptums were sitting in two lawn chairs watching a middle school choir belt out patriotic songs.

The two younger men, Remember Knott and DieWell Barebones were seated in the local coffee shop, *The Burned Tongue,* which advertised coffee hotter than MacDonald's and stronger than Stallone.

"Stallone?" Mary Rose asked, looking at the sign in the window.

"Sylvester," Robbie said. "He wanted to be the strongest man, the richest man and the best actor in the world."

"Two out of three ain't bad," Marge said, opening the door. The girls sat at a table near Remember and DieWell. Hadley went to the counter to get decafs for her friends.

"What would you like, Ma'am?" the young man behind the counter asked.

"What I would like is a triple shot of vanilla in a strong latte, but what I'll take is four decafs, no cream, no sugar."

The young man smiled at her, "Lady, you are a barista's dream!" He poured the coffee into four colorful mugs, put them on a tray, then carried them to her table. He asked the two Puritan descendants if they wanted refills and they both nodded.

"Have you two seen the Bahl brothers?" Marge asked Remember and DieWell. "They seem to have gone missing."

The two men looked at each other. "They were at the B&B this morning," DieWell said. "Harry ran out in the rain and Buster went after him a few minutes later."

"Are those old farts running off with a couple of old broads?" Remember asked with humor in his voice. "More power to 'em!"

The two men talked about living together in Iowa City after meeting in a coffee shop there. Both their great grandfathers had been instrumental in creating a flourishing Salem's Crossing and they thought the Puritan Reunion would be a fun mini-vacation. They were pleasant and chatty and seemed to genuinely like the BOOB Girls.

Marge gave them her cell phone number and asked them to call her if they came across the Bahls.

Matilda Minor-Milldew

She was a six-foot tall Amazon and no one gave her any trouble. No one made any wise cracks, at least where she could hear, about her baseball cap with "Chief" embroidered in pink across the front. No one mentioned her black sneakers with pink curly laces, and no one ever said anything about her collection of Vera Bradley handbags which hung on the coat tree in her office. No one gave the police chief any trouble at all.

She was beautiful, big and powerful. The only one even close to her in the intimidation department was Marge Aaron and the two law-enforcement women got along just fine. They understood each other.

Geoffrey seemed to understand everyone, better or worse. He was sitting beside Chief Matilda's chair, waiting for her to sit, stay and rub his head.

The chief was pouring strong and bitter coffee, a prerequisite for all police departments, into five white Styrofoam cups sitting on five pink napkins on the battered table in her reception area.

"Actually, I'm divorced," the chief was saying in answer to a snoopy question by Mary Rose McGill. "Once I joked to my ex, 'We've been through a lot together. Most of it was your fault.'"

She put the coffee pot down on the table. "He accused me of being a new divorced black Barbie doll, one that comes with all of Ken's stuff, but actually we split things pretty 50/50 except he claims when it came to the house I got the inside and he got the outside."

"Divorce is a grief in and of itself," Hadley said. "My son has been divorced tree times. Then he finds another woman. I think the unhealthiest thing he eats is wedding cake."

Matilda nodded. "Marriage is a great institution, but only if you like being institutionalized. Let's face it, marriage is the leading cause of divorce. But seriously, I wonder how we could have been so in love and then fallen as far out of it as we were when we fell into it. It's sad and it's a death, death of a relationship, death of a love.

"The big difference is in divorce you don't have a corpse and he doesn't disappear to leave you a clean shot at living. He's always there. We run into each other. A friend dies and we're both at the funeral. People with kids have it even harder. You just have to cry sometimes and other times make sure your sense of humor is up and running" She sat down and looked at the girls. "What's up?"

"A house full of Puritans, two of whom are missing," Robbie said.

"The Bahls have vanished," Mary Rose added.

"You might say we are women without Bahls," Hadley smiled.

The chief looked at Marge. "Then there are the Puritan dolls…" Marge explained about how the men had left without a trace and then the two dolls had vanished as well. "I just called Scooter at the B&B and neither Bahls nor dolls have reappeared. She actually seemed to not understand what I was talking about."

"We couldn't find the two men anyplace in town." Mary Rose said.

The police chief looked around and sighed. "Bummer," was all she said, reaching for the big mastiff head waiting beside her chair.

They stood. "They haven't been gone long enough to be worried, but we are," Hadley said. "It's just a weird feeling we all have."

The chief nodded. She knew about weird feelings. "We'll trust our intuition and see what we can find."

Red-Tail Two

The drive back to the B&B and their trailer was quiet. Even Geoffrey kept his head inside in the air conditioning and didn't smudge up the window in a subtle hint for someone to roll it down. Chief Minor-Milldew had promised to do all she could and was staying late at her office researching Bahls.

The Hummer pulled silently into the circle drive in front of Scooter's place. All the other cars were there, including Harry Bahl's, untouched, its windows still rolled down. The puddles had dried around it and the car looked lonely, forlorn and old.

The field of grain across the road shivered and shimmered in the heat. The wind was totally still. Only a solitary cicada could be heard practicing its mating call.

"Oh, look," Mary Rose said, pointing to the sky over the field. "Isn't that beautiful?" Circling in gracious and ever-increasing ovals was the red-tailed hawk.

"You don't see those very often in Nebraska," Marge said.

"No," Hadley said, clutching her arms as if hugging herself. "But Wes and I always saw them at his cabin and I loved their call. It's wild and spooky and would scare the fur right off a rodent. I saw it catch a snake this morning."

Just then, the great bird circled the girls, tipped its wings as if in greeting and shrieked the "Eeeee'ahhh" call of a powerful predator. They all watched it as it sailed over the field, its red tail glimmering in the late day sun.

"It was kind of our bird, Wes' and mine," Hadley whispered, tears bouncing into her eyes.

"Very cool," Mary Rose said, missing the tears.

They went inside to say good night to Scooter.

Eight little Puritans brightest under heaven,
One hurt her neck and then there were seven.

Seven little Puritans cutting up their tricks,
One went to sleep and then there were six.

They let Geoffrey sniff around the yard. It was too hot and humid for him to run much. Hadley had turned the air conditioning on in the trailer so things would be cool when they went in. They had been outside for about fifteen minutes. More cicadas had joined the chorus and crickets were competing for top billing.

"You know," Robbie said. "I'll be glad to settle into our trailer. I just feel a little uneasy about being here, period." The Bahl brothers disappearance was worrisome.

They were sitting in lawn chairs outside the trailer door. The awning over the side of the trailer was rolled down, the outdoor carpet had been put in place and the entire space was cozy and enjoyable.

"I know what you mean," Hadley said. "Something is just not quite right."

"Ditto that," Marge added.

Mary Rose looked at Marge. "Marge you're a good cop. What do you think is going on?"

"I don't' have a clue, Mary Rose. And I mean that literally – there are no clues to where the Bahls went."

"Well, I know where I'm going," Mary Rose said. "I don't have to go back inside the house to pee. I'm going to visit our new facility." She got up stiffly and began to walk to the pink outhouse. Geoffrey followed her.

The girls folded up their chairs, slid them under the trailer and went inside. The last sounds of the warm summer night were of Mary Rose shutting the trailer door behind her when she returned, a doggy tail hitting the wall inside with its best wag and the gentle groan of the trailer awning motor as Mary Rose pressed the button that wound it up for the night.

Above them, the full Buck Moon of July shown down, signaling it was time for antlers to push out of the young buck deers' foreheads. A barn owl asked, "Who?" In just minutes the lights in the trailer blinked off and all was still.

The Next Vanishing Act

The air conditioner had run all night. Robinson Leary woke up tired. It was always difficult for her to sleep when she could hear a motor running. Hadley had suggested she think of it as the trailer purring like a cat. Robbie didn't particularly like cats.

In fact, they all looked a little worse for wear as they gathered in the kitchen just before seven to serve a continental breakfast to the guests. Each of them had grabbed a cup of coffee the minute they walked in. Scooter had been up for three hours and looked disgustingly fresh.

"I am *never* going to live with anyone again," Marge was saying. "When I look at myself in the mirror first thing in the morning, it's Revenge of the Rat Woman."

"Don't blame yourself, dear," Hadley said, patting Marge on the back. "I have a haunted apartment. When I look in the mirror in the morning, this ugly old lady jumps in front of me and I only see her reflection, not mine." They laughed.

"I don't let even the mirror see me," Mary Rose said. "And remember, some days I put on Depends!"

"I don't look in the mirror until after I get my hair dried and my makeup on. I am NOT a glutton for punishment!" Robbie looked at her friends, all grinning at her. "I say what we need is some *SHIT*!"

It was not the usual cuss word. This was their signal to pay attention to their posture. *Shoulders back, Head high, Eyes (I's) straight ahead Tummy tucked in.* They all straightened up and for at least a few minutes had remarkably good posture.

"Quit using bad language in my kitchen when we have guests!" Scooter stuck her head out of the pantry for a second, and then pulled it back in.

Breakfast passed without incident or Bahls. No one had seen them or heard anything about them. They were not a hot topic for the group gathered around the big table.

"Oh, Scooter," Patience Evenow said, pushing her chair away from the table. "Do you know a good chiropractor? I slept wrong and my neck is so stiff I can hardly move it." She twisted her shoulders to demonstrate the immobility.

"Nope," was Scooters compassionate reply.

None of the other guests could help. "Oh well," Patience sighed. "I'll go get Abstinence and we can drive up to Wood River. I bet there's one there. Abstinence is sleeping like a baby. I envy that!" And she stiffly but with determination made her way out of the dining room to the stairs leading to their room, carefully carrying a cup of steaming coffee and sweet roll for her sleeping roommate.

They cleaned up the breakfast dishes, wiped off the huge dining room table and said goodbye as guests left for another reunion day. Ella Simptums helped with the cleanup. Once again she was dressed in a stylish jogging suit and after Hadley's question said that she, too, did a lot of volunteering. She had also met Penstemon and told Hadley that she, herself, was having some memory problems "I just get fuddled and confused," she said.

"I've never heard it said better," Hadley replied.

As Ella Simptums walked out the door and took the arm of her husband, Robbie went to the mirrored table and began to count. Hadley joined her and very shortly both Marge and Mary Rose came over, questioning looks on their faces.

"Two of the women dolls are gone," Robbie said. "Two men, two women." They looked at each other. Ken David David bounced in the front door after a quick morning run with Geoffrey. He gave them all a cheery wave.

"Ken David," Marge said. "How many cars are outside?"

"That's easy," Ken David said, roughing up a happy Geoffrey. "Mr. Bahls old classic and that new one those two ladies were driving." He sat down, cross-legged on the floor next to Geoffrey. The mastiff gently laid his big head in the boy's lap. "Boy," Ken David David went on, playing with Geoffrey's ear, "Geoff sure doesn't like old Mr. Stolzfoo's black stallion."

The girls turned as if they were a drill team and started up the stairs toward the room assigned to Abstinence and Patience. It was empty, the two beds neatly made, clothes carefully hung in the closet.

"They're gone," Mary Rose said. "Just like the Bahls and just like the dolls."

Downstairs, Scooter patted first Geoffrey and then Ken David David. "Just between us, Ken David, those four burned out old broads are the craziest I've ever seen. I can never make any sense out of what they're up to." Ken David nodded in exact time to Geoffrey's tail wagging.

"Scooter, we're going into town to look for the ladies and the Bahls," Marge yelled, grabbing her red cane as they hurried down the stairs.

"Ken David David, take care of Geoffrey," Mary Rose shouted, and the girls bumped into each other in their rush toward the door.

"Lots of luck," Scooter mumbled. Ken David David nodded. Geoffrey asked why he couldn't go Ride, too, but no one paid any attention to him.

Mary Rose was first down the porch stairs, followed by Marge who headed down the ramp to humor her knee that acted up. She was balancing her red cane on her left arm and holding on to the ramp banister with her right hand. Robbie stepped carefully down the stairs and Hadley followed close behind her.

As they scurried toward the Hummer parked beside the house, Hadley stopped short and looked at the ground. There, lying with their quills crossed were two beautiful red feathers, released from the tail of the red-tailed hawk. Hadley picked them up and tucked them ever so carefully into an outside pocket of her purse. She looked around, apprehensive that she might find the big bird dead somewhere. It was too unusual to find two feathers in one spot without a tragedy behind them. "Any of you see the red-tailed hawk?" she called.

Immediately Robbie pointed straight up. "There, Hadley. He just landed."

Seated high above them in the top limbs of the giant oak, green leaves shining in the sun like dragon scales, the hawk was barely visible through a space between the branches. There sat the majestic bird, watching through bright black eyes, its beak open as if ready to speak. Hadley breathed a sigh of relief and climbed into the front seat beside Marge who had pretty much taken over as permanent chauffeur.

"Remember when we were here last fall," Mary Rose said, "and the birds we saw were all big crows?"

Hadley fingered the feathers in the pocket of her purse. "You're thinking about Wes, aren't you?" Robbie asked softly from the back seat.

Hadley nodded.

Coffee with the Chief

"I swear," Robinson Leary was saying, "next year, next story, we are STAYING IN OMAHA! I am not coming out here again. In fact, I don't care if I NEVER see Salem's Crossing again." Sweat had formed on her forehead, her sneakers were dusty and she felt grimy all over.

They parked in front of the little supermarket, each took an aisle and searched the grocery store for four missing Puritans. All they found were slightly over-priced groceries.

Hadley had jumped out of the Hummer and peered into the window of The Burned Tongue Coffee Shop. The passengers in the Hummer were hopeful when she dashed inside but lost heart when she hurried back out, carrying only a tray with four cups of decaf.

The laundromat held only clean clothes and young apartment dwellers. A long shot at the *Rack Your Balls Pool Hall* yielded balls but not Bahls. *Anita Trim,* the local beauty shop was a bust as well, but made Robbie mumble, "Where do they get these names?" once more.

They drove slowly up and down the streets of the little town. They cased the senior center and even stopped at the local mortuary, but decided that was way too long a long shot. Finally, tired and hopeless, they settled for a piece of pie at Finicky Frank's restaurant. That's where they found the police chief, Matilda Minor-Milldew.

The chief was seated at a back table in the restaurant, a steaming cup of coffee on the table by her side, her laptop computer open in front of her. An empty pie plate was pushed toward the end of the table and the chief was concentrating and squinting at the computer screen.

"Chief," Marge said in way of a greeting as they all sat down at Matilda's table.

Marge hooked the red cane over the back of her chair and set her purse down beside her.

"Girls," the chief replied, closing the top of her computer and lifting her coffee cup in greeting. Her baseball hat with "Chief" embroidered in bright pink was hung tenderly over one arm of her chair. Her green and yellow Vera Bradley bag lay at her feet like a loyal puppy, the top zipper open.

Looking around, Hadley noticed the same woman who had been typing away at Shut Up and Drink was busily typing away now at Frank's. This time, she was reaching for a steaming mug of coffee without looking. She took hold of the handle while still typing with her right hand, lifted the mug to her lips for a sip and put it down again without missing one key on the keypad. Hadley was impressed.

The waitress came over immediately. Hadley moved her head to let the powerful air conditioning cool her sweaty forehead. "What'll ya have?" the server asked. She was a veteran, tall, tough and muscled. The old dudes at the bar knew better than to give her any grief.

Robbie looked at her name tag and dropped her head to the table. Mary Rose looked up and grinned. "Leigh," she smiled at the server "Leigh VaTipp." She pointed to herself, "I'm Mary Rose, this is Marge, Hadley, and the one with her head on the table is Robinson and, of course…" she pointed to the chief.

"I know the chief." Leigh tilted her head toward Robbie, "She OK?"

Mary Rose smiled. "She just likes your name."

They each ordered a different pie: apple, peach, strawberry rhubarb, cherry and the chief ordered a second piece of pecan. The pie here is the best in town," she said.

It was Marge's turn to smile. "It's the ONLY pie in town."

The chief nodded. "And what brings you in to *make my day*? I love it when Dirty Harry says that, but it always sounds different coming from me."

Hadley doubted that even Dirty Harry would stand up to Matilda Minor-Milldew. For one thing, he only came up to her shoulder and she looked a lot better with a gun on her hip than he did.

"Anything on the Bahls?" Robbie asked. She had lifted her head and stopped laughing.

"Nothing. I went out to the fishing resort and Brenda hasn't seen them either. She's a nice lady. Scooter should partner with her and get along, but getting along with Scooter is hard. You can't get on her good side because she doesn't HAVE a good side."

"That's from *Steel Magnolias*," Robbie muttered in appreciation. "And you're right. Scooter is getting grumpier and grumpier, even the bed and breakfast seems grouchy. No one has signed up for meals other than the continental breakfast we have every morning."

"We have another situation," Marge said. The pieces of pie arrived along with decaf and a refill of regular for the chief. For one bite they were silent, and then Marge continued. "The older ladies are missing – Abstinence Evermore and Patience Evenow. No trace. Just like the Bahls. All their belongings are in their rooms and we've scoured the town."

"The dolls are missing, too," Mary Rose added. She was more fascinated with the missing dolls than the missing Puritans.

"If this is like the Agatha Christie story," Robbie said, "the poem should fit the mystery as well." She pulled a folded piece of paper out of her purse. She had copied the poem in Scooter's home office. She began to read it aloud.

> **"Ten little Puritans dressed up so fine,**
> **One walked on water**
> **and then there were nine."**

"Yo," Hadley said. "It was pouring just before Harry Bahls went outside to roll up his car windows. He had to have 'walked on water.'" Robbie nodded and read the next stanza.

> **"Nine little Puritans sure they would be late,**
> **One hurried off and then there were eight."**

Mary Rose jumped up a tiny bit in her chair, she was so excited. "Buster Bahls dashed out of the house looking for Harry and saying we would all be late for the stuff going on at the senior center. Read the next one, Robbie."

**"Eight little Puritans brightest under heaven,
One hurt her neck and then there were seven."**

It was Marge's turn. "Patience said she had slept wrong and her neck hurt. She asked about a chiropractor but there are none in town."

Matilda pulled out her cell phone. "There's one in Wood River. I go to her." She dialed a number and spoke for just a minute with whoever answered. "They haven't been there or called the doctor's office."

"I've got the next one," Robbie said.

**"Seven little Puritans cutting up their tricks,
One went to sleep and then there were six."**

She looked at the other women, "I don't know about the 'cutting up their tricks', but Patience went upstairs because she thought Abstinence was still asleep. She apparently had a late night." She read the rest of the poem:

**"Six little Puritans playing with a hive,
A bee stung one and then there were five.**

**Five little Puritans drinking in the bar,
One passed out and then there were four.**

**Four little Puritans up on a spree,
One got fuddled and then there were three.**

**Three little Puritans with a hot dog and brew,
One spilled his ketchup
and then there were two.**

**Two little Puritans lying in the sun,
One got too hot and then there was one.**

**One little puritan being all alone,
That one ran away and then there were none."**

"Sweet Jesus," Marge said. "The dang thing fits!"

"That line about drinking in the bar," Matilda said, "could mean we need to alert Hummer over at Shut Up and Drink to call us when one of them comes in, or at least keep an eye on him or her."

"And that line about being 'fuddled,'" Hadley said, leaning in toward the center of the table. "Ella Simptums used that word when she got confused about something that first morning." She looked around the table. "Fuddled."

They were quiet for a time. Chief Minor-Milldew wiped her forehead with the fingers of her right hand. "There is something about Abstinence Evermore that rings a bell." She opened her computer, turned it on, and then typed rapidly.

Robbie's cell phone rang. She looked at the caller ID. "I have to take this," she said. Everything was quiet except for the gentle clicking of Matilda's computer keys. "I know," Robbie said, nodding her head. "I know – even though expected, it's always a surprise." There was a pause. "I don't think it's denial, Max, it's mind-wrapping. It seems impossible to wrap your mind about the fact he'll never come back, never be there, that he's gone forever."

A tear made its way out of her eye and down her cheek. Matilda stopped typing. "I love you, too. Keep on keeping on, girlfriend." Robbie hit the END button and slipped her phone into her purse. They looked at her.

"My cousin Connie died," she said. "I only have cousins for family, you know." She sighed. "Cancer. I didn't see him a lot, but we talked now and then and we loved each other. He was funny and sweet and loved his granddaughter so much he was determined to live to see her graduate from college. He had such faith. He KNEW he was going to make it. He didn't. His wife says she thinks the treatment as much as the disease killed him."

Her expression changed and she leaned forward to look more directly at her friends. "I tell you here and now, girls, if I get a cancer diagnosis, I'm going to just enjoy the time I have left. No chemo. No radiation. I mean it!"

They were quiet for a minute, then Marge spoke up. "You'll probably die of a heart attack where you conk out immediately, kiddo. Me, I'll die from knee pain." She became serious. "I have a cousin dying, too. His name is Larry. Again, cancer. It's a frigging epidemic." They all nodded.

Hadley spoke up. "Like the old duke in Lord Snowdon's documentary said, "The most difficult part of growing old is, by all means, the death of one's contemporaries." They all nodded again.

The chief broke the sad silence. "I'm going to look up our two missing ladies, Abstinence and Patience and see if there are any records of them on the law enforcement websites." Conversation started up. Life went on over pie and coffee.

"Got something," Matilda said, after just a few minutes. "Our Abstinence was at one time the highest paid call girl in Omaha, flying on corporate jets, getting trips to Europe and around the world. She was indeed, as the poem said, 'cutting up tricks,' And guess who her 'manager' was."

The girls looked at each other, then altogether said, "Patience Evenow."

"Bingo," Matilda said, "seems these ladies modeled themselves after Anna Wilson, Omaha's first and

most famous madam. They even have a website and
here's what they say:

**'When we die, we wish to be remembered as
is Anna Wilson, who is buried in Prospect Hill
Cemetery in Omaha. She is a folk legend. a
madam who generated great respect.'**

**'She was the mistress of Dan Allen, a river boat
gambler. She invested in real estate and became
a millionaire before her death in 1911. She
donated her brothel, a huge mansion with porch
pillars carved as naked women, to the city as an
emergency hospital.**

**'She lived to be seventy-six and was buried
next to Dan under nine feet of concrete so the
'respectable' society women of the town couldn't
dig her up and move her out of the cemetery."**

"Interesting," Robbie said, pushing back from the
table and crossing her legs. "Anna was admired by
a lot of the 'society' women who used her and her
girls as a means of birth control. One journal said
they would nod in appreciation to her when they
met her on the street. When their husbands wanted
sex and they were afraid of becoming pregnant,
they sent them to Anna. She and Dan Allen are
buried together in the nicest graves in Prospect Hill
Cemetery. At one time she owned most of the land
downtown where ConAgra, the old libraryand the
pedestrian bridge are now."

Mary Rose shook her head and looked at Robbie then at Hadley, "How does she know all that stuff?"

Hadley spoke up, "I know a little about her. She truly loved Dan Allen, the gambler, and she spent a fortune in fresh flowers which she put on his grave every day for years. She lost a true love when he died…the love of her life."

Hadley looked down at her coffee cup then quickly took a sip.

"Like you and Wes," Robbie said, touching Hadley's hand. "Like you and Wes."

Hadley nodded. "Kind of," she said softly.

"Well," Marge said, pouring more coffee from the pot Leigh had put on the table. "that may solve the mystery. Two old galoots have run off for some hanky-panky with two old hookers."

Matilda smiled. "They may not show up for a while. Old dudes like that are pretty slow."

Robbie laughed. "I watched Fritz Coleman on YouTube. He's a weather man. He says men always think about just one part of their bodies." She made a circle with her hand over her pubic area. "When they're young they think about sex every three and a half minutes. When they're old, they think about finding a bathroom every three and a half minutes."

"Weather man?" Mary Rose asked. She was going to say more, but Hadley didn't give her time.

Hadley leaned forward again and broke in. "At Meadow Lakes, going to a urologist is a rite of passage for a man moving in. He goes to the urologist and if his wife goes with him, she sits in the doctor's office, leafing through magazines and grinning because for years she's gone to an ob-gyn, stretched out on the table and looked at instruments laying right underneath the air conditioning vent and she's thinking, 'It's your turn now, buddy.'"

Leigh VaTipp came over to ask if they needed anything else and to find out what was so funny. "Old people sex jokes," Matilda answered, putting her money – including a tip – on the table. The others followed suit.

"You ladies want to meet for an early dinner at Shut Up and Drink?" Matilda asked. "I may have a lead or two on our fearsome foursome of two old men and two old ladies by then."

They agreed. Shut Up and Drink had great burgers. As they left Finicky Frank's Stonewell Stolzfoos' black horse and expensive black carriage rattled by occupied by four boisterous Puritans attending the reunion. They waved to the girls who could hear their laughter from their spot on the sidewalk.

"That's the first time we've seen anybody in the carriage," Marge observed with a serious look in her eyes, "the first time."

They piled into the Hummer. Mary Rose looked at her watch. "It's still early girls. What do you say we find the fishing resort and visit Brenda Lee Colton? We may find a cabin with four sexy old people hiding in it."

Marge peeled out of their parking space and headed northeast toward the river and Scenic Point Fishing Resort.

Fishy, Fishy in a Brook

The last two miles to the fishing resort were gravel road. Dust rose in huge clouds behind the Hummer, coating its back window. Hadley thanked God for air conditioning and they talked about the days before AC when you rolled the windows down and let hot air blow through the vehicle and then got out windblown and sweaty.

On the way, they passed a beautiful little abandoned church, small and white with a steeple reaching toward Heaven. Carriage tracks led up to it and the black horse and carriage were tied to an old-fashioned hitching rail at the side of the church.

"We're too far past, now," Robbie said, "but if Stonewell's carriage is there when we come back, let's ask him if he's seen our two boys and two girls."

"He probably arranged their little get-together," Hadley said. They laughed.

The Scenic Point Resort was indeed scenic. Nine modern, attractive cabins faced the Loup River, its current wending its way toward the mighty Missouri. They parked the Hummer in front of the large log cabin that served as office and restaurant. As they got out, the wind chased its tail in a dust devil in front of them. Heat bore down from a summer sun. As they climbed the steps to the front door, it was opened by a smiling Brenda Lee Colton. "Welcome!" she said in a cheery voice. They went inside to a comfortable coolness.

Seated in oversized wooden rocking chairs in front of an unlit fireplace were three white-haired ladies. "These are my aunts," Brenda said, spreading out her arm toward the ladies, who smiled and nodded at the girls but didn't get up. "I'll get us some ice tea," Brenda added, and disappeared into the kitchen.

"I'm Maggie, the first woman said from her rocker. "Next to me here is Opal and over there we have Laura. What are your names?"

Mary Rose made introductions. Brenda came back with a tray of ice tea and cookies which she sat on a huge coffee table. The girls pulled up chairs from the dining room table and made a circle around the tea. The big living area was cozy and comfortable, with a rustic interior that fit the countryside perfectly.

"We have a question, Brenda," Marge began, "have you seen or rented a cabin to two elderly gentlemen named Bahls and two older ladies, names of Evermore and Evenow?"

Brenda shook her head. "I'm full up, including a children's author, but no one fits that description. Do they need a place to stay?"

"We think they've run off together from the bed and breakfast," Mary Rose added.

"Sex scandal!" Aunt Maggie hooted. "And they're experienced. They're old."

"It's amazing what you can still do when you're ancient," Opal said.

"They'll have to go some to beat us," Laura said with conviction.

"My aunts used to change husbands more often than they changed socks," Brenda said, passing out the tea and cookies.

"What about Mr. Stolzfoos?" Robbie asked. "Has he taken any of your renters for a ride around town?"

"Not that I know of," Brenda replied. "But he must be doing well. I see the carriage a lot."

There was a noisy barking at the door and four little dogs dashed in. "Whoa! Jazzmine!" Brenda pointed to the floor and they all scurried over and lay down at her feet. "Ladies, meet the beasts. Elvis is the poodle, Winchester is the German Shorthair, Remington is a Hungarian Vizsla and so is Benelli." The dogs panted and wagged and gave off doggie happy vibes.

"But you said 'Jazzmine' like it was a command," Mary Rose said.

"Jazzmine was the cat. She died at age fourteen, but she ruled the roost. All I have to do is mention her name and these four behave. I wish I could say the same about my aunties!"

Dr. Pawter, DVM

"I like her," Mary Rose said, as they climbed back into the Hummer. Just before they started to drive off, Robbie's cell phone rang. "When? Give me an address." She began to punch an address into the Hummer's navigation system. "We're on our way." They looked at her, eyes full of interest and questions. "It was Ken David. We've got to get to the vet, a Dr. Pawter. Geoffrey's been stung by more than one wasp."

Marge sped out of the driveway at Scenic Point. Robbie looked over her shoulder at Hadley and Mary Rose in the back seat. "But the big thing is that Ken David said Remember Knott and DieWell Barebones are missing," she paused. "And so are two more Puritan dolls."

"Geoffrey is more important than those two Puritans!" Mary Rose said in a loud voice. Her face was lined with worry and she was twisting her hands.

"It will be OK, Mary Rose," Hadley said, reaching for her hand. "He's a big tough dog. No flying insect with a stinger is a match for our Geoff." Mary Rose nodded, but she didn't seem convinced.

Marge pushed the Hummer farther north on the gravel road. In a short time the navigation system in the big vehicle told them they had reached their destination. A large sign at the lane leading up to a beautiful old farmhouse read:

Jane Pawter, DVM,
Specializing in Geriatric Mules, Old Dogs,
Zinnias and Flying Squirrels.

"Versatile," Robbie said. They could see Scooter's old Chevy in the drive in front of the house. They parked, got out and hurried to the front door. Mary Rose beat them all there and rang the bell. No one answered. She rang it again then pounded on the door.

Ken David David's voice came from behind the house. "We're back here, ladies."

They rushed around the house. Everywhere they looked were beautiful zinnia beds in full bloom, every color of the rainbow and more. They had obviously been planted and cared for with love and tenderness. The whole place seemed happy.

In the back was a large stable, the front of which was a vet's office. Coming out the back door of the house was the doctor, a woman of medium height with brown hair and sensible shoes. She was wearing a stained white lab coat and carrying two steaming mugs, one in each hand. She wore bright red lipstick and walked incredibly fast. The girls actually trotted a little to catch up with her. Not a drop of liquid in the mugs splashed out.

"I'm having a late lunch," the doctor said over her shoulder. "I drink coffee in the morning," she held up the mug in her left hand, "and tea in the afternoon." She held up the other mug. "I just have time for the coffee before I switch to tea."

"Is that some weird health thing?" Marge whispered loudly to Robbie. Marge's red cane was bouncing along on her arm as she hurried. Robbie shrugged and breathed harder.

They all reached the doctor just as she reached the office door. Ken David David held it open and they hurried in. Geoffrey lay on a table, obviously lifted there by Ken David, who stood close to him, rubbing the dog's head, talking to him and looking worried. Geoffrey was looking at the boy, but there was no happy tongue or joyful wagging going on.

"I'm sure he'll be OK," Doctor Pawter said. "I've applied ointment to the stings and given him a shot. Luckily, there were no stingers left in his skin. Now we're going to get to the tricky question." She took a sip of her coffee and placed both cups on a shelf by the table where Geoffrey lay.

"The tricky question?" Mary Rose asked, moving beside Geoffrey and rubbing his big shoulder. His tail gave one wag when he realized she was there.

"Ken David says he tries to poop and can't get anything out. He strains and strains and gets a funny look on his face, but no results."

"He was always a good pooper," Mary Rose said. Ken David David nodded.

Hadley smiled, "The funny look was just his normal face."

Dr. Pawter put on rubber gloves and went to Geoffrey's rear end. An elderly mule, wanting to know what was going on, poked her head out of one of the stalls and peered accusingly in their direction.

"Aha ha!" the doctor said. "My word, how did he swallow this?" She lifted Geoffrey's tail and was taking a careful look under it. "Wait till you see this, ladies!"

She reached under the big tail and began to pull something out of Geoffrey's rear. She pulled and pulled, gently but steadily.

"Sweet Jesus!" Hadley said.

"Good God Almighty," Robbie said.

"Jesus, Mary and Joseph," Mary Rose said.

"No shit!" Marge said, "No pun intended."

Dr. Pawter was pulling a huge piece of rope out of Geoffrey's behind. The mastiff had a surprised and relieved look on his face.

"That is huge!" Marge said.

"Poor baby!" Mary Rose said.

"Whatta guy!" Ken David said.

"I don't believe it," Hadley and Robbie said together.

"I wouldn't have believed it if I hadn't seen it myself," the vet said. She grabbed her coffee mug and finished the strong liquid in a couple of swallows, then reached for the tea. Bright red lipstick marked both mugs.

She walked a few steps to a big sink and carefully soaped and washed the rope. There were two small knots in it. She dried it in an air drier on the wall, and dropped it in a large plastic zip-lock bag. "Here's the strangest souvenir you'll ever have," she said, handing the bag to Mary Rose.

"Thank you for bringing him out, Ken David," Mary Rose said gratefully.

"Let's see how he's feeling," Jane Pawter said, looking at Ken David. "Lift him off, honey."

Ken David put his arms under Geoffrey and, bending his knees, picked up the mastiff and placed him with a gentle thump on the floor. Geoffrey looked around, grinned and bounded toward Mary Rose, who leaned down and kissed his head.

Just as she was straightening up, a little black and white fuzz lump of a dog bounced between Mary Rose's feet, walked quickly underneath Geoffrey who looked down between his legs, his ears standing up, his head almost touching the floor.

"Che!" Doctor Pawter smiled. "Here." She bent down, held her arms open and the little dog did a flying leap into them. Che is a Havanese, national dog of Cuba." The vet stroked the little head. "Hasn't ever been able to swallow a rope."

The doctor walked out with them. Geoffrey ran toward the Hummer, Che right behind him.

"The zinnias are gorgeous," Hadley said. "But what about the flying squirrels mentioned on your sign?" "Just wait a minute," Jane said. They all stood totally still. Then, from a tree above came the rustle of leaves and a small brownish-grey squirrel spread it's little webbed legs and glided, rather than flew, to a treetop several feet away.

"Sandhill cranes and flying squirrels," Robbie said, faking a hillbilly accent as they got into the Hummer. "It don't git no better than Nebraska."

"And one red-tailed hawk," Hadley thought with a tender smile.

They had just gotten out of Dr. Pawter's driveway when Mary Rose jumped up a little off her seat, "We totally forgot about Remember Knott and DieWell Barebones."

"It's time to meet the chief at Shut Up and Drink," Marge said. "Maybe one of them is like the poem and passed out in the bar."

The hot day followed them in a dust cloud down the gravel road toward town. Geoffrey was sound asleep in the back, Mary Rose was thinking how grateful she was that he was okay, Hadley was still wondering if she would see the red-tailed hawk again and Marge and Robbie were thinking about how precious cousins could be.

Six little Puritans playing with a hive,
A bee stung one and then there were five.

Five little Puritans drinking in the bar,
One passed out and then there were four.

As soon as Mary Rose tied Geoffrey to a post on the porch of Shut Up and Drink, he flopped down, looked at her with one eye for a few seconds, then went sound to sleep, snoring before she even turned away.

The bar was cool with a smell of old furniture polish and the last remnants of smoke before Nebraska passed no smoking ordinances. The chief of police was at a table near the center of the tavern, her computer open, her Vera Bradley bag on the floor by her feet. Her chief's hat was pushed back on her head, revealing a row of tight black and grey curls.

Hadley looked around, noticing once again the woman who was typing furiously in a far corner. She stopped typing, put her head in her hands, moved her fingers over her forehead and appeared to be thinking. Brenda's children's author? The one she had mentioned when they visited her?

Hadley stood still and swept the tavern with her eyes, then she pointed to the bar. There, with a large glass of beer in front of him, was DieWell Barebones, the missing Puritan, complete in his Puritan costume. The girls went to Matilda's table. Marge draped her red cane over the back of a chair and headed toward DieWell.

Robbie and Hadley filled the chief in with details of Ken David's phone call telling them Remember and DieWell were missing, along with two additional men dolls. Mary Rose told her about Geoffrey getting stung and trying to digest a rope. The chief tut-tutted in sympathy.

Marge returned to the table, a somewhat tipsy DieWell following her, his large Puritan hat in one hand, a fresh beer in another. "Ladies!" he said, with just a slight slur in his voice. He pulled up a chair from a table next to them, and all the women leaned forward, looking at him. He responded with a puzzled expression. "What?" he said.

"Tell us what happened to Remember, DieWell." Marge said. "He seems to have gone missing, or at least Ken David thinks so."

"Oh," DieWell took a drink of the frosty cold beer while Humiliation the bartender came over with glasses of chardonnay for Hadley and Robbie and beers for the chief and Marge.

"Remember was helping Scooter get rid of a wasp's nest on the corner of the B&B. Well, rather, he was knocking it down while Scooter supervised." He looked around at the women. "That old broad can be just a little grumpy, you know." He took another swallow of beer. "Like they say, 'No good deed goes unpunished.' Remember knocked the wasps down and the nest wasn't empty like Scooter said, it was full of the little bastards." He hiccupped, excused himself and apologized for his language.

"Remember ran like he was on fire, dashed into the woods. The bugs took after old Geffrey, and last I saw of them, Remember was headed in this direction at full speed and Ken David was chasing Geoffrey, yelling for him to stop. The poor old dog was running like he was constipated or something." He looked at them and grinned. "I figured Remember was coming here, so I came here, too. But he hasn't shown up yet."

"You make a good looking Puritan," Hadley said with a smile, while she admired DieWell's costume.

"Yeah, well the costume's too hot and I'm not into religion." He held up his glass. The cold drinks tasted good to everyone at the table.

"If you ask me," DieWell said, "beer is better than religion." He raised his left hand and started counting off fingers.

1. No one will kill you for not drinking beer.
2. Beer has never caused a war – a fistfight or two, maybe, but never a war.
3. Beer doesn't tell you how to have sex.
4. They don't force beer on minors who can't think for themselves.
5. When you have a beer, you don't knock on people's doors and try to give it to them.
6. Nobody's ever been burned at the stake, hanged or tortured over his brand of beer.
7. You don't have to wait 2,000 years for a second beer.
8. There are laws saying beer labels can't lie to you.
9. You can prove you have a beer.

He stopped, looked at the ceiling and thought for a second or two. "There's one more……..I got it!

10. If you have devoted your life to beer there are groups to help you.

He gave Marge a friendly slap on the shoulder and laughed. They laughed with him.

"For my next performance, I plan to go to the bathroom." He stood up and staggered to the men's room. It was a long time before the girls realized he hadn't come back.

Chief Minor-Milldew had found nothing new on Abstinence and Patience or the Bahls brothers. The girls told her about visiting Brenda and the Scenic Resort and seeing the black horse and carriage at the old church. Mary Rose took out her lipstick and applied it to her lips. "Looking good, girlfriend," Robbie said.

"I get up every morning and do damage control," Matilda said.

Hadley looked at Mary Rose and smiled. "Give her the speech, Mary Rose."

Mary Rose leaned forward in her chair. "It is our very strong opinion, Matilda, that older women are beautiful." She cleared her throat. "Just look at us! Our faces are sculpted and chiseled by joy and sorrow, tears and laughter, our hair is blown thin by winds of experience and there is so much knowledge and wisdom in our heads, our heads can't hold it all so it has to trickle down to the rest of our body. That's why we get thicker as we age."

Matilda laughed.

Marge leaned forward, "And what's most important, chief, is we know SHIT!" She pointed to Robbie who sat up very straight.

"**S**houlders back, **H**ead high, **I**'s (eyes) straight ahead, **T**ummy tucked in. **SHIT**. It reminds us to watch our posture. They all straightened up in their chairs. For older ladies, at that moment they had remarkably good posture. As they were talking and laughing, Stonewell Stolzfoos' black horse and carriage rambled slowly by Shut Up and Drink. Geoffrey lifted his head and growled, but no one heard him.

Matilda looked at her watch. "I want a burger."

They all nodded and Marge beckoned Humiliation over to their table. All at once her face became serious. "Holy Cow! How long has DieWell been gone?" They all looked at their watches.

"Too long," the chief said, and she and Marge made a dash for the men's room. Matilda threw open the door. "Police!" she yelled. Two young men came running out, one zipping his pants the other leading the rush toward the front door. Geoffrey gave a short bark as they jumped past him.

Bring on the Cavalry!

The only thing new when they returned to the Bed and Breakfast was that Penstemon Primrose had missed her afternoon nap, Scooter was grouchier than ever, and now there were only four Puritan dolls left on the mirrored table, two men and two women. Marge looked at her friends. "Go out behind the outhouse, ladies. I'll meet you there in a minute. We need to do some serious cane practice."

They looked mildly confused but did what Marge said. In just minutes she came out the back door, a bag of tin cans in her hand. She went to the fence behind the pink outhouse and lined up cans on the square posts. She walked back to the girls, limping slightly.

"I don't ever plan to be without the cane," she began. "But in this situation, it wouldn't hurt for all of you to learn how to use it. Just pass it around for a minute and get a feel for it." Loaded, it was considerably heavier than a normal cane.

Marge walked slowly toward the trailer. They hefted the red cane, turned it over in their hands, passed it back and forth. Very shortly, Marge returned with a white bed sheet from their linen closet.

"We'll put this down when we push the jewel for tripping pellets. They're hard to come by and I don't want to lose any." She spread the sheet in front of Hadley.

"Which jewel do you want to try first, Hadley?"

"Tripping pellets will be fine," Hadley said, lifting the red cane like a rifle. Marge lowered it. "We're going to trip the bad guys, honey, not put out their eye." She pointed to one jewel. Hadley pushed it. The red cane bucked just a little in her arms and pellets quickly spread out and landed on the sheet.

"Cool!" Hadley said. She pushed another jewel and a taser beam shot out, barely missing Marge, who jumped to one side.

"Sorry about that," Hadley said, handing the cane to Robbie.

"Pick up the pellets, Wild Bill," Marge said. Hadley picked up the pellets.

Robbie took the red cane. "Show me the rifle," Marge pointed to a jewel.

Robbie aimed at one of the cans on the posts, pressed the jewel and absorbed the kick of the rifle. The can flew off the post.

"Good job!" Marge said. "You can push any jewel and be all right, girl."

Robbie handed the red cane to Mary Rose.

"Taser," Mary Rose said. Marge pointed to the taser jewel. Mary Rose reached around the red cane as far as she could and pressed a jewel. A knife flew out on each side of the red cane. Mary Rose squeaked.

"Mary Rose, you can do this!" Marge stood back just in case. "Try it again."

This time Mary Rose used her other hand to hit the jewel. This time the smoke screen went off and filled the air with thick fog. Mary Rose coughed.

"One more try," Marge urged.

Mary Rose held the red cane by her side, studied the jewels and pressed one. A taser beam shot into the ground.

"Close enough," Marge said with a sigh.

They practiced for what seemed a long time, Hadley watching the sky for her hawk while the others studied the art of red caning. Blackbirds swarmed into the trees, talking their good nights. She could hear robins having conversations, but not one hawk or other predator soared above them or gave a hunting call.

Well before dark they were worn out. They headed for the big porch surrounding the Bed and Breakfast.

They poured themselves glasses of ice tea and settled in on the porch with the big rockers. Scooter brought her grumpiness along and joined them. Mary Rose had a thoughtful look on her face. Hadley noticed it when she turned her head, still hoping to see the red-tailed hawk. "Penny for your thoughts, girlfriend."

Mary Rose looked at her. "I was looking at the ramp the boys built for Alphonso and I miss Wiley. I miss Wes, too, Hadley. I was thinking that Wiley and Alphonso would really enjoy Scenic Point and some good river fishing."

"Humph!" Scooter snorted.

"Call Brenda and see if any of her guests have left. She may have a cabin open up now that the weekend is over." Hadley suggested.

"Humph!" Scooter said, louder this time.

Mary Rose googled Scenic Point on her smart phone and hit the CALL icon. Brenda Colton answered on the second ring and Mary Rose asked if she had a cabin. She listened, smiled, nodded, gave thumbs up to her friends and finished her conversation.

"She doesn't have a cabin, but she has a ground floor room in the lodge that is handicap accessible. I'm going to see if they want to come."

She called Wiley Vondra. They wanted to come.

And they came the next day, with a cloud of dust and Willie Nelson blaring from Alphonso's van. The dust was raised from the road in front of the Bed and Breakfast, and Willie Nelson sounded as if he were trying to out sing the two men inside the van. The windows were rolled down, even in the summer heat, and the girls and Scooter could hear the noise from where they were sitting and waiting on the front porch.

The boys were like two teenagers with their stereo blaring full blast and their windows all open. Ella Simptums came hurrying out the door with Ophelia Payne close behind her, both looking down the road to see where the sound was coming from. Royal Payne and Sam Simptums opened the screen door almost as soon as their wives had let it slam shut.

"Caterwauling!" Royal Payne said. Ophelia glared at him. It seemed she glared at him every time she looked at him.

Alphonso pulled the van up in front of the porch steps. Wiley jumped out and hurried to the back of the vehicle where the doors were already opening revealing the platform that lowered Alphonso's scooter, The Mean Machine. In just minutes Alphonso was headed toward the ramp. He was seated like a king on the scooter. Geoffrey was running happy circles around the two men, hitting Wiley in the knees with his wagging tail.

The lift was slowly retreating inside the van, Soon the doors would automatically shut. "Listen to this," Wiley called out. He moved beside his friend and threw an arm over his shoulders. Together they started whistling The Fishing Hole Song from the old Andy Griffth Show.

Robbie leaned toward Hadley, "We're being serenaded."

Hadley grinned. "Is that what you call it?"

The girls laughed, Mary Rose clapped her hands and the four BOOB Girls hurried down the steps for hugs and cheek kisses. All four were somewhat surprised at how good they felt now that the two old dudes were there. It was sort of a joyous safe feeling, like the Cavalry had just ridden into town and the bad guys in black hats had better skedaddle.

Wiley had his arm around Mary Rose's shoulder and Marge had her arm around Alphonso as he sat on his scooter. "You girls should have seen the hawk that escorted us in," Wiley said.

"Biggest red-tail I ever saw," Alphonso added.

All the girls looked at Hadley who nodded and smiled, moving in to take her turn at hugs. Robbie was close behind and to their surprise, Scooter joined the group. "Ice tea before you goes to that witch's retreat? Can't tell you boys how glad I am to see you. This place needs the presence of manliness and that manliness has obviously just arrived along with a good dose of common sense and intelligence."

All four girls did eye rolls. Robbie thought she was a little too flowery and sweet all at once. She didn't like it. She looked at Marge who did a second eye roll and obviously didn't like it either.

Scooter was back to her normal unpleasant self as soon as they settled around the big dining table with their tea and some cookies Scooter had picked up at the grocery store.

The girls spent a good hour bringing Wiley and Alphonso into the loop, interrupted only by Scooter's "Harrumphs" and "Ha's!" as well as much head shaking and the making of ugly faces, some of which were hard to distinguish from Scooter's usual appearance.

They told the boys about the disappearing Puritans. Robbie went to the mirrored table, brought the poem over and read it aloud, pointing out what had happened that matched each stanza. They told Wiley and Alphonso about Chief Matilda Minor-Milldew and her web searches. Wiley had begun to look sleepy until Hadley got to the part about Abstinence being a high-priced call girl with Patience for a manager and how they loved Anna Wilson.

"I laid a flower on her grave once," Wiley said in an aside to Alphonso. Alphonso nodded approval.

"How do you women get yourselves into situations like this?" Alphonso asked, looking at Marge who was seated next to him. There was just a hint of criticism in his voice. Then his face broke into a grin and he said in a loud voice, "I love it!"

"What if they've all been killed though?" Mary Rose asked. She was starting to put her hands together, then release them, as she did when she was nervous.

Wiley reached around in front of her and held her hands. "If something bad had happened, Mary Rose, we would have heard. Now, The Fonz here and I, are going to spend some quality time fishing. You all stay here, or go in for pie or see the chief for whatever. We'll be back about four and we can all go to Shut Up and Drink and have an early dinner." He stood up and tried to look important. "The guys in white hats have ridden into town! There's a new sheriff," he said, pointing to Alphonso.

Marge smiled. "When you go to Scenic Point, watch for Stolzfoo's black horse and carriage, will you?"

They walked out to the van where, once again technology served Alphonso well, lifting him and The Mean Machine into the back. They saw him move into the driver's seat, Wiley moving in to ride shotgun. The boys waved. The girls waved back and the brave heroes headed north to terrorize some innocent fish that had done nothing worse than make the Loup River their home.

"What now?" Hadley asked. "If we're staying here, I have a book on my tablet I want to finish. I'll sit on the porch and watch for the red-tail."

"I think I'll take a nap," Marge answered. "I didn't sleep well and I don't want to fall asleep in my sandwich at the tavern."

"I have some things to look up on the computer," Robbie said. "And I think I'll google all our guests and see if anything interesting comes up." They looked at Mary Rose, who had a suspicious-looking smile on her face.

"I'm going to crawl into the moose head and see what I can see."

From the Eye of the Moose

Mary Rose McGill found the secret door in the hall that led to the moose head. She opened the door, put her knees on the little padded stool that allowed someone to lean forward and stick her or his upper body into the moose head, pull back the panel on the eye and see what was happening below.

Mary Rose knelt on the stool, reached behind her, pulled the door shut and stuck her head into the moose. "Crap!" she mumbled. She was too short. She squirmed around, her nose almost touching the door, opened it and peeked out. The hall was still and empty.

She tiptoed to the first bedroom, the one belonging to Patience and Abstinence. She knocked just in case. As expected, when there was no answer, she went inside and grabbed two pillows from the beds. She hurried back to the secret door in the wall.

The pillows worked. It took some doing, but she balanced them on the stool, pulled herself up by hanging onto the wall that had been opened up to hang the head, and was able to crawl inside a little while keeping her knees on the pillows. It wasn't bad. In fact, it was warm and cozy, like being bundled up in winter clothing on a cool day. Though the day outside was hot, the moose head was cooler and only smelled a little. It was a sweet, soft, old smell like a cherished old dog. Mary Rose opened the panel over the eye and looked down.

She could see the dining room, the table, the fireplace. She could see more than she had imagined. It was interesting and exciting. Then it was boring. Mary Rose heard the big grandfather clock strike the quarter hour, then the half hour. She had begun to nod just a little when the Paynes, Ophelia and Royal, came into the dining room to pour themselves glasses of ice tea. They were arguing, and then Mary Rose realized the dining room had really good acoustics.

"Yeah, well we would make a really good team if it weren't for you!" Royal was almost yelling at Ophelia, as he poured one glass and added ice from the silver bucket sitting nearby.

Ophelia grabbed a glass and shook it at him. "Most of what we've been through is entirely your fault!" Ophelia yelled back. "I should poison you!" She was gripping the glass so tightly that Mary Rose was afraid it would shatter.

"If you gave me poison, I'd drink it! Bring it outside, woman! I'll be catching some rays in the front yard."

Ophelia moved around and took hold of the back of one of the dining room chairs. Mary Rose wondered if she was going to pick it up and smash it over Royal's head.

Royal took a step back, turned and took hold of another chair. "Do you know the meaning of WIFE? It means Without Information Fighting Everytime."

"Wrong! It means With Idiot For Ever! Marriage is when one is always right and the other is the husband!"

"Why do you always have to have the last word?"

"Becaus,e if *you* have the last word, it's just the beginning of another argument."

Royal started for the door. "One thing for sure," he said over his shoulder, "marrying you gave me religion. Before I married you, I didn't believe in Hell!"

Ophelia started after him. "Royal Payne," she growled. "I am going to kill you!"

Mary Rose listened, fascinated. After a few minutes, she watched Geoffrey bounce into the dining room with Ken David David behind him carrying three stolen slices of lunch meat. Ken David sat at the table; Geoffrey did a world class 'sit' beside him.

Ken David let a slice of the lunch meat hang out of his mouth and Geoffrey chewed it until their lips met. The other two slices got broken up into smaller pieces and they shared them. Mary Rose watched them and smiled. Sometimes love just needs a big dog to show you that life is more than lunch meat.

Mary Rose laid her head down on the moose's neck, the panel in the eye still open. She could hear Ken David talking softly to Geoffrey the mastiff who was beating a steady rhythm on the floor with his tail. It was comfortable inside the moose head. It was comfortable hearing Ken David's voice. It felt safe there, as though no one would ever bother her again. Mary Rose McGill drifted off to sleep listening to a boy talking boy talk to a big loving dog.

Penstemon Primrose, the little lady with dementia, passed gracefully through the now-empty dining room on her way to her afternoon nap. Mary Rose slept on. Geoffrey came in and stretched out on his favorite spot in front of the fireplace. After a time, a hand reached out to the mirrored table that held the Puritan dolls and quietly lifted two dolls into a small bag. The arm was recognizable and disappeared in seconds. It had been in plain sight, but Mary Rose McGill was still asleep.

When she woke up, groggy and somewhat confused, imagining hearing her name being called from a long way away, she looked out through the eye of the moose to see her three friends looking up at her and waving their arms.

"We know you're up there, McGill!" Marge said, leaning gently on her red cane.

"I have a glass of wine bet that you went to sleep," Robbie said.

"Get your tiny heiny down here, girl. We're meeting Wiley and Alphonso at Shut Up and Drink," Hadley called up to her. "A Rueben sandwich and a tall glass of wine have my name on them!"

Mary Rose stuck a finger out of the eye, did a finger wave at the girls and began to unwind herself off the pillows and stool. She felt slow and stiff.

"I have to go to the bathroom," she said as she entered the dining room. She had carefully put the pillows back on the other ladies' beds and hurried downstairs to her friends. "I need to pee and like the chief; I definitely need to do damage control to my hair."

"It's not everyone who gets moose head instead of bed head," Hadley smiled. As she turned to grin at Robbie, she noticed that only two Puritan dolls were standing by the lamppost on the mirrored table. "Uh, oh," she said, pointing.

**Four little Puritans up on a spree,
One got fuddled and then there were three.**

**Three little Puritans with a hot dog and brew,
One spilled the ketchup and then there were two.**

Shut Up and Drink was packed. They squeezed around a table at the tavern, telling Wiley and Alphonso about the two additional missing dolls. Marge, her red cane balanced carefully on the back of her chair, called Chief Minor-Milldew and Matilda strode in the door shortly after they had ordered sandwiches and drinks. She pulled up a chair and nodded and smiled at the boys. They met last year shortly after the ramp for Alphonso's scooter had been finished.

"What do we have?" the chief asked.

"Absolutely nothing," Wiley said. "Even their telling us hasn't helped answer any questions."

"It seems strange," Alphonso added, "how the poem goes along with the vanishing Puritans. That takes a hell of a lot of planning."

"And look at the next two stanzas," Robbie said. "Four little Puritans up on a spree. What does that mean?"

"Yo!" Wiley said. "That's why this place is so full. There's a poster at the fishing resort advertising a "Puritan Spree, Suds and Scrabble Contest here at the tavern. I noticed several tables had Scrabble set up. I thought it was just an everyday thing."

Humiliation Strykes came over with a towel over his arm, ready to take the chief's order.

"Hummer," the chief asked. "Anybody in here get confused or what she would have called 'fuddled'? And anyone spill any ketchup?"

Hummer grinned. "Everybody in here gets confused." He squatted down by Matilda and looked up at her. "There was one lady, in her Puritan dress. I remember her because her outfit was really well done and authentic. She got confused about where she had left her purse after she had eaten her hot dog. She was headed out to check their car and this man bumps into her husband. The guy is holding a bottle of our ketchup and it splashes out all over the poor husband. I offered to wash it off his shirt but he said his wife was headed for the car; he'd just go to the B&B and change. That's the last I saw of him."

"The Simptums," the girls said together.

"Did you also see Stolzfoos' carriage?" Marge asked.

"Oh, I see that all the time," Hummer said. "What'll ya have top cop?" He stood and touched Matilda on the shoulder.

Hummer left to get Matilda a soda. They were quiet for a while.

"I know one thing I'm going to do," Robbie announced, standing up and pushing her chair back. "I'm going to find out who our mysterious writer is."

The woman with the laptop was once again typing away in a corner of the tavern, oblivious to the entire crowd around her. Robbie wound her way through the tables, pulled up a chair next to the woman and sat down.

Nancy and the Mud Eaters

"Hi, my name is Robinson Leary and we couldn't help noticing how busy and concentrated you were. May I ask what you're writing?" Robbie wore her brightest, friendliest, you-can-trust-me smile.

The lady stopped typing, leaned back in her chair and took a sip of her Stella beer. "I'm Nancy Sothanski, and I've just started a new series of chapter books for middle school kids." She returned Robbie's smile. Nancy was definitely not dressed as a Puritan. She had on white slacks and a Nebraska Cornhusker golf shirt. Her red sandals matched her shirt and her brown hair fell gracefully behind her ears.

"Really!" Robbie said, genuinely surprised. "I taught English literature at Creighton."

"I love the Blue Jays," Nancy said, referring to Omaha's favorite basketball team.

Robbie took a long look at her. "So your name is Sothanski – not something like Shadow SoThin or anything weird, just a plain all-American name?"

Nancy looked puzzled. "Right. Teaching lit on a college level, you probably haven't heard of my other books, all for young people. I wrote the *Max and the Mud Eaters* series. I wrote *Rosie, Ruthie and the*

Rebellious Reptiles series and now I'm starting a new series. This one will be the *Grandma Belle* series where a feisty little grandmother who is like four foot nothing, gets kids to help her solve mysteries. She's tough and nobody messes with her."

Robbie nodded, impressed. "Where are you staying, Nancy?"

Scenic Point, but I need people around when I write. I come here or I go to Finicky Frank's. People sounds comfort me. I write better." She nodded toward Wiley and Alphonso. "I saw the two elderly gentlemen at your table over at the resort. Actually, I'm from Bellevue, and this was supposed to be a getaway to write, but then I ran into all these Puritans."

"We're actually looking for some Puritans." For some reason known only to women, Robbie told her new friend all about the missing Puritans.

"That's a mystery that's book-worthy," Nancy smiled. "I don't know if it's helpful, but I drive in every day and something weird is going on at the old, abandoned church between here and Scenic Point."

"Stonewell's carriage there sometimes?" Robbie asked, leaning in close.

"Sometimes, but Stonewell the Amish doesn't seem to be driving it. Some weird guy in a Puritan suit seems to be trying to hide his face every time I see him. I did get a glimpse of his tee shirt one day, before he slipped another shirt on over it. On the back it said, 'Butch Sleezer's Fertility Clinic.'"

Robbie shook her head. "Oh, come on! Who would own a business with a name like that?" she asked no one in particular.

Nancy answered, "Butch Sleezer?"

Robbie shook her head and came back to reality. "And you had such a nice, ordinary name – then here comes Butch Sleezer and a fertility clinic." She looked at Nancy. "Will you come over and tell all of us what you think is going on?" Robbie stood up and pointed to the already crowed table where her friends were watching her.

"Sure," Nancy said. "I'm not sure anybody knows what's going on but it's time for a break and I bet you'll buy me another Stella."

She squeezed into a spot between Hadley and Marge and told them about seeing a lot of activity in the old church. "It may just be a part of this crazy reunion." She said. "I hear that at six o'clock tonight," she looked at her watch, "that's in about ten minutes, they're going to fire the canon on the square and set off fireworks to commemorate the Puritan founding of Salem's Crossing."

Nancy told them about the man driving the carriage and how his tee shirt read "Butch Sleezer's Fertility Clinic." Wiley and Alphonso loved it. "You know what it really is," Wiley said, leaning toward Mary Rose.

Mary Rose leaned away from him and said, "What?"

"Butch inseminates hogs. I bet he has a slogan like 'Butch's Boars are Best.'"

Alphonso chuckled. "I bet they have a state-of-the-art Lab-BOAR-a-tory there, too."

Matilda began to laugh and the whole table followed suit, causing Scrabble players nearby to look at them and frown. Hummer came by and asked if they wanted another round. Just then the canon went off with a bang and a boom in the town square. The tables shook. The sound of fireworks drowned out all conversation.

"Well," Marge said, running her fingers over her red cane. "If I were going to shoot anybody, I'd do it right then, during those fireworks. No one would notice."

Robbie's cell phone rang.

"It's Scooter. She's mad. She wants to know what we've done with all the Puritan dolls."

"All?" the girls asked together.

"The last two are gone now," Robbie answered. She picked up her purse and dug in it for the poem.

Two little Puritans lying in the sun,
One got too hot and then there was one.

One little puritan being all alone,
Had to run away and then there were none.

"OMG!" Mary Rose exclaimed, "Royal Payne said he was going to 'catch some rays' in the front yard." She looked around at them. "That means he was going to lay out in the sun. And the way Ophelia was talking to him and looking at him…" There was a pause. "I think she's killed him. Shot him during the fireworks like Marge said." Mary Rose said it so softly they could barely hear her.

"That's a tad far-fetched, Mary Rose," Matilda said, smiling at the group. "I imagine, at the very worst, she's run away from him. And the whole poem may be inaccurate. It's a bit too much for me. I want you folks to just have a normal evening," She picked up her nearly empty soda glass and leaned back in her chair. "Let's finish our drinks and you can do whatever you want to do. Later tonight I'm driving by the church to see if Stonewell or the Sleezer tee shirt is there. As for now, I need a beer and I'm off duty." She waved to Hummer who knew what she wanted.

People were beginning to leave the tavern. Penstemon Primrose came in and ordered a Jack Daniels. Robbie's cell phone rang again.

"Scooter," Robbie said, looking at the caller ID. She put the phone to her ear and listened and nodded. She hit the end button. "She wants us to come back as soon as we can and help her make sandwiches. She's catering a picnic at the church tomorrow and needs thirty sandwiches."

"I guess that means the church is part of the reunion celebration," Nancy the writer said. "I'm going to hit Finicky Frank's and see if I can get another chapter of Grandma Belle done." She smiled at Marge. "My Grandma Belle would fit right in with you ladies."

Part Three

Take Her Back!

Five Deadly Terms Women Use When Arguing with Men

Fine! This is the term a woman uses to end an argument when she knows she is right and you need to shut up.

Nothing means **Something** and you need to be worried.

Go Ahead! This is a dare, not permission. Do Not Do It!

Whatever: A woman's way of saying, 'screw you.'

That's Okay: She is thinking long and hard on how you will pay for your mistake.

Wow! This is NOT a bonus word. She is wondering how any one person could be so stupid.

They all six crowded into the kitchen at the Bed and Breakfast and under Hadley's organization, made ham sandwiches, chicken sandwiches, egg salad sandwiches and cucumber sandwiches. in case a vegetarian was on the loose as a Puritan. Scooter stood in the doorway and yelled orders and demands.

When they finished, they each ate one sandwich, accompanied by only moderately cool soda from Scooter's refrigerator. Scooter, who had barked and bossed and growled and grunted and chased Geoffrey out of the kitchen, had gone to bed in a huff, not even thanking all of them for helping.

"I am so not coming back here," Robbie announced. "The next story is all Omaha. Scooter has some serious issues. I think insanity doesn't run through her family, it wanders through slowly, takes its time and gets to know everybody."

"The fishing resort is great," Alphonso said, reaching over and patting Marge's knee that had been bothering her because she had stood so long. The sandwiches would be picked up in the morning, but no one cared. Marge's cane lay casually on the dining room table. Geoffrey was snoring softly at Mary Rose's feet.

"I don't even care that all her guests are gone," Mary Rose said, "and that is most unkind."

"They probably took one look at Scooter and just left until the reunion is over and then they'll come back for their stuff and argue about paying their bills," Hadley added.

Marge struggled to her feet, leaning carefully on her red cane. "I don't know about you five, but I'm breaking out the wine."

The grandfather clock struck the hour. Four minutes later, Marge came out of the kitchen with a bottle of red and a bottle of white, set them on the table and went to the cupboard for glasses. Wiley stood up and poured. Hadley went into the kitchen and magically returned with a plate of cheeses and saltine crackers.

"Humble, but good," Alphonso said. They raised their glasses. "To friendship and to us," They all took a sip and dug into the cheese. Mary Rose looked intently at Wiley.

"What?" Wiley asked, looking back at her and licking cracker crumbs off his lips.

"You are a good-looking old dude, Wiley Vondra." Nancy the writer had called the boys "old dudes" and Mary Rose liked the sound of it.

Everyone looked at Wiley and smiled. He chewed his cheese and cracker and grinned a sheepish, youthful grin.

"I'm serious," Mary Rose said. "And, Alphonso, you are a handsome old dude, too."

Robbie grinned wider. "I like what Fritz Coleman, the weather man, says." She cleared her throat. "He says something like, when a man gets old, his face says, 'I'm tired of being a face. I think I'll be a chin,' and it slips down and waggles in front of his neck. His chest says, 'That's a good idea. I think I'll move south and become a stomach, then those firm, strong thighs melt like tapioca and run down his legs until they meet resistance, then they bounce up a ways and become swollen ankles.'" She leaned forward and looked at the two old men. "Nope, you guys didn't do that. You are indeed two handsome old dudes."

Alphonso and Wiley looked at each other and didn't have a clue what to say. Finally, together they said, "Weather man?"

"I will say, though," Hadley smiled, "Wes had you both beat. He was the tall, dark and handsome guy who literally wore the white hat. This is about the time, with all these missing Puritans, that we would call in the sheriff." She looked at her friends and lifted her wine glass. "To the sheriff," she said softly.

"The sheriff," they repeated and touched their glasses together.

They talked some more about the missing Puritans: the Bahl brothers, Patience Evenow and Abstinence Evermore, Remember Knott and DieWell Barebones. They wondered aloud about Sam and Ella Simptums and the Royal Paynes.

Marge reached for her red cane where it lay on the table and began to check to see if the taser, rifle, smoke screen, tripping pellets and knives were charged and ready to go. She checked the gold lariat in the handle, as well. Everyone was talking about the Puritans and they hardly noticed her preparations.

"I still think they've just gone off somewhere. If someone had killed them, there would be bodies showing up all over the place," Hadley surmised.

"Not necessarily, girlfriend," Marge said. "This is farm country. A body could stay hidden between rows of this corn until harvest comes if no one wonders about the birds circling around, then it would be nothing but bones."

"How about the river?" Mary Rose added, determined to make things as deadly as possible. "Bodies could be under that water or miles downstream."

"In the town where I grew up, we had a lake, and a man name Plum drowned himself in it. For weeks we said we were drinking Plum Water," Robbie said, then she added, "I don't believe I said that! It's not only insensitive; it's a crazy name like the ones that bug me."

Mary Rose stood up. "I'm headed for the trailer and bed. The thing I think I hate most about getting old is how danged tired I get!" She covered her face with her hands and sneezed violently. "On the other hand, now that I'm old, I can multitask. I can laugh, sneeze and pee all at the same time."

She went around the table for hugs. Hadley and Robbie cleaned up the glasses and dishes, Mary Rose and Robbie walked out the door with the boys and as the last rays of light dropped over the western horizon, the red-tailed hawk landed gracefully on the roof of the weary old mansion and in the shadow of a gargoyle, closed its eyes and tucked its head under its wing.

Mary Rose McGill went to sleep as soon as she crawled into her bunk. Geoffrey was taking up a good share of the bed as he lay at her feet, curled up as tight as he could curl and watching her with big, loving brown eyes. His other women had laughed softly, talked together for a few minutes then taken turns in the bathroom before turning in.

Geoffrey was listening in the quiet. There were so many sounds here away from the city. He could hear a raccoon circle the trailer. A skunk slipped by. Geoffrey couldn't hear the skunk, but he could get a whiff of the sharp, strong scent the animal carried with her wherever she went. Crickets were singing and, every so often, a night hawk would sound its deep call as it dived for food.

Geoffrey was still listening when he heard the hoof beats of the hated horse stop in front of the house. He was still listening when Robinson Leary climbed down from the bunk above his Mary Rose. Robbie mumbled something about, "drinking wine before bed" and went into the bathroom. The big dog listened as Mary Rose woke up, got up, saw the light under the bathroom door and knew it was occupied. She did a little hop. "Dang it! I gotta go!" She looked around, desparate. "Outhouse!" she whispered, slipping into her slippers.

Geoffrey poured himself off the bottom bunk, back legs following his front end like slow moving liquid, and padded after his favorite lady to the door of the trailer. She didn't take him with her. The screen door shut hard, almost hitting his big old nose. She hadn't even noticed he was there.

Robbie shuffled out of the bathroom, her eyes only half open. She didn't notice Geoffrey looking out the door. She didn't notice that Mary Rose was not in her bed. When Geoffrey heard the sound of a struggle and a stifled scream that came out more like a squeak, he growled the deepest, meanest growl he could muster. He barked once, as loud as he could.

"Quiet, Geoff!" Marge said from the other bedroom. "Good dog." Her voice was slurred with sleep. Geoff looked around. Finally he lay down in front of the door and waited.

And waited.

And waited.

Everything outside was quiet. Even the crickets weren't making any noise.

He was still waiting the next morning when his other three women got up and came into the kitchen to make coffee. He didn't move. They didn't seem to see that his favorite woman wasn't there anymore or that he never lay like this in front of the door looking out and waiting. Sometimes humans are not the brightest stud on the dog collar.

Missing!

"Girls! Look!" Robbie said, pointing out the trailer window with her coffee mug. "The sandwiches are being picked up by old Stonewell or his helper that Nancy the writer mentioned."

They crowded around the window, peering out at the thin man in a Puritan outfit who was loading the box of wrapped sandwiches onto the floor of the carriage and climbing in behind them. He picked up the reins and the horse headed for the road.

Hadley looked around. "Mary Rose must have gotten up really early and gone into the house to help Scooter." They looked at the empty bed as if they could find her there.

"If she did, she didn't dress first," Marge said, pointing to the clothes Mary Rose had carefully hung on a hanger to wear the next day. "No housecoat, no jammies and most of all, her bed isn't made. Have you ever known Mary Rose McGill to NOT make her bed? She joked once about making the bed while her husband was still in it." She looked at the dog who had stood and growled when he heard the horse approach and kept on standing when he heard his mistress's name. "Where is she, Geoffrey? Where's your lady, boy?" Marge asked.

Geoffrey barked once, whined a most pitiful and sad whine and looked out the screen door.

"Shit!" Marge said. She didn't mean for them to straighten up, either. She meant get out the door and find her fast. They rushed out the door, Robbie nearly falling over Geoffrey who bounded out and headed to a spot near the outhouse. When he saw the women were racing to the house, he bounced after them, ready to see Mary Rose whom he loved best.

"Where is she, Scooter?!" Marge had grabbed her red cane and was pointing it at the little lady with white bed head who was pouring her own cup of tea in the trailer kitchen.

"Who?"

"Mary Rose! What have you done with her?" Robbie nearly yelled.

"She's missing," Hadley said, the fear creeping into her voice.

"Haven't seen her." Scooter took a sip of her hot tea and sat down at the dining room table.

"We saw the Amish carriage here," Robbie said.

"Picked up the sandwiches," Scooter snorted.

"The church!" Marge yelled and they bumped into each other heading for the door.

Geoffrey was the first out, determined to track Mary Rose. Hadley caught on.

"Where is she, Geoffrey? Good dog. Find Mary Rose."

They followed him around the trailer. They watched as he went to the outhouse and sniffed. The door to the outdoor toilet had been left open and swung weakly on its hinges.

When Geoffrey bent his big head to the ground a few feet in front of the old outhouse, all three women moved toward him. Marge had her cane in her hand, Hadley was grasping her robe closed and Robbie was hopping on one foot after stepping out of one slipper.

"Here, boy," Marge said, bending toward Geoffrey.

When Geoffrey turned around, held tight in his teeth was a piece of rope, exactly like the one he had eaten just days before. Hanging out of one corner of his mouth was a torn piece of Mary Rose's pajamas. Marge took ahold of the rope and torn triangle of fabric and Geoffrey let go, allowing fabric and rope to slip into her hand.

"Let's go, ladies," Marge said. All of them, including the big mastiff, hurried up the trailer steps and rushed inside to grab clothes. Marge grabbed her cell phone from its charger near her bed and dialed Alphonso's number. "Meet us at the old church, now! Mary Rose has been kidnapped!" She hung up before Alphonso could say anything and grabbed her slacks from yesterday. Within ten minutes they were in the Hummer, Geoffrey's head out the window, a determined look on his big awkward face, headed north toward the old church.

It was Hadley who had called the police chief who would meet them at the church, telling them she would come in slow and silent, no sirens.

"Kidnaped"

They all arrived at the same time. Marge and the chief pulled the Hummer and the police car into the church driveway, blocking any escape for the horse and carriage parked at the side of the church. Alphonso pulled his van in behind them. There was no way out. By the time the girls were out of the Hummer and Matilda Minor-Milldew out of her cruiser, pistol drawn, Alphonso was on his scooter headed up the ramp to the front door of the church, Wiley Vondra just steps ahead of him. As they neared the door the first notes of a hideous bell choir sounded what they thought might be "Amazing Grace." They all stopped short.

"Break the door down," Hadley said to Marge.

"Break the door down," Marge said to Wiley

"I have a better idea," the chief said over the sound of the bells. She stepped forward and simply knocked loudly on the door.

The music stopped.

There was total silence, then footsteps headed toward the door. A key was turned, a latch was lifted, the door opened and Mary Rose McGill stuck her head out.

"Oh, good! You're just in time for bell practice. Come on in. We have fresh rolls from the bakery and sandwiches for later."

Get Me to the Church on Time

The little church sanctuary looked crowded. There were sleeping cots along the walls, bedding neatly folded beside each one. Nearly all the people, however, were on the stage up front where an old pulpit had been rolled out of the way. Hadley and Marge both did a quick count and decided twenty kidnap victims were crowded into the small space on the stage, each with a bell in hand.

Geoffrey made a beeline toward Mary Rose, sat at her feet and looked up at her with adoring eyes. "I was an excellent detective," Mary Rose said, smiling at Marge, who held her red can firmly in her hand. "I found a coil of rope. I found the bells and organized a bell choir or a chime group or whatever you want to call it," Mary Rose explained. "The Bahls insist on naming it Belles with Bahls but I don't really like that. The trouble is, the Bahls brothers have the biggest bells and if they don't get the name they want they won't play." She shook her head. "So far, I'm afraid, they argue and fight more than they practice."

"Mary Rose," Robbie said, "You've been here overnight and you've organized a bell choir of kidnap victims?"

Mary Rose nodded. "We also captured our kidnapper and tied him up with the rope I found." She pointed to a spot just past where Alphonso sat on his scooter. The man with the Puritan costume and tee shirt advertising Butch Sleezer's Fertility Clinic was tied to a chair with a gag in his mouth, his hat at an angle on his head. Beads of sweat were running down his forehead and into his eye, causing him to continuously shake his head.

"He went for the sandwiches and I learned the Bahls had worked at one of the Lincoln taverns as bouncers when they were young," Mary Rose explained.

"Don't tell me," Robbie said, shaking her own head. "They called themselves The Bouncing Bahls."

Mary Rose looked at Hadley, "How does she know that stuff?"

She pointed to the Puritan with the gag in his mouth. "He was fired from Butch Sleezer's Fertility Clinic for stealing boar sperm and selling it on the black market, that would be the Black Boar Market." Mary Rose giggled and put her hand over her mouth. "The Bahls tackled him when he came in the door with the sandwiches. Harry even grabbed the sandwich box with one hand, while he held him with the other, so we didn't lose one sandwich in the scuffle. He saved our lunch."

Matilda Minor-Milldew had holstered the gun she had drawn when she first arrived. "Stealing boar sperm. You don't hear that charge every day."

"He's Stonewell's nephew and he talked poor mister Stolzfoos into taking a vacation in Kansas so he could tie Puritans up and kidnap them and *throw them in the carriage!*" She said the last words very loudly, leaning in toward the subdued kidnapper. Even in her torn pajamas, Mary Rose looked threatening.

"He was going to ransom us to the town," Mary Rose continued. The arguing from the bell choir made an irritating and continual background noise as she talked. "He even had a note prepared." She walked over to a bulletin board on one wall and too off a sheet of paper, carefully sticking the thumbtack that held it back into the corkboard.

They gathered around and Matilda read the note out loud:

I kidnaped 20 of your good citizens

Leave $20 thou in a bag by the canon at noon and you will get them all back.

If you don't you won't
See them agin.

"Oh, for Pete's sake!" Robbie said, pointing to the note. "Look at that misspelling. He didn't kidnap them he kid-nayped them. There are two 'p's in kidnapped and two 'n's in cannon and he left an 'a' out of 'again."

They looked at her. Mary Rose put her hand on Geoffrey's head and shook her finger at the kidnapper. "And he's the one who left the rope for our poor Geoffrey to eat and then not be able to poop." Geoffrey looked at Mary Rose, drooled and wagged his tail. The noise from the unhappy bell choir was continuing.

"These people are terrible victims," Mary Rose said. "They insisted on all kinds of good food, games and special treatment and they refuse to leave until after they've had their sandwiches." She looked around, "Speaking of special treatment, Abstinence and Patience have been welcoming old men from town ever since they got here. They've taken over the church parlor.

"Remember Knott and DieWell Barebones, on the other hand, have spent the time forming a new lawyer-banker business and I think they'll do really well. The Simptums have rediscovered each other and are acting like honeymooners. And the Bahls, well Bahls will be Bahls." Just then Harry Bahls threw a large bell at his brother's head, hitting it hard enough to cause a bruise and a bump. There was more ringing and yelling.

"Quiet! Police!" Matilda yelled. "I want everybody sitting down on their cots and getting ready to make a statement." She walked over to the tied up kidnapper and pulled out his gag.

"What's your name?"

"Finnegan Farquhar," the man spit the name out into the air. "And she's right. These people are terrible victims! And take her back! She's the worst of all. I'm never kidnapping her or any of them again. Can you guess what it cost me to feed them? One night they made me get prime rib to go from Finicky Frank's."

Matilda began to untie the kidnapper. "You have the right to- -" Before she could get to the end of the sentence, Farquhar had jumped up from his seat, knocked the chief to the floor, thrown a chair at Alphonso, who was closest to him, and headed for the door.

Mary Rose grabbed Marge's cane, aimed it at the escaping kidnapper, yelled, "I've got him!" and pressed one of the cane's jewels. A massive cloud of choking smoke billowed into the room, burning eyes and blinding everyone.

"Don't do that, Mary Rose!" Marge yelled, grabbing the cane back. "You know you never hit the taser button!"

"I really thought I had it this time," Mary Rose said, shaking her head sadly.

Geoffrey shook his head to clear it from the smoke. He could see better than the humans, and he saw the funny man dash out the door. He saw Alphonso start his scooter and chase after the funny man. "Run!" Geoffrey thought. "Play! Run!"

This would be better than chasing rabbits. His long doggie legs had him at the door in seconds, right after Alphonso. While the big man drove down the ramp, Geoffrey jumped high off the top of the church steps and took off after the funny man. "Run! Play!" He passed the fleeing kidnapper in no time and was running merrily down the road in front of him.

"Geoff! Get him!" Alphonso yelled. He was gunning that old scooter and gaining on the man. Geoffrey stood in the middle of the road and watched. In no time at all, the man was blocked by a huge dog and the former Kansas City Chief's linebacker was diving through the air to tackle the funny man. This was fun! Play!

Alphonso landed on Finnegan Farquhar with a thunderous thud, dust springing up around them. "Here, Geoffrey," Alphonso called. He held the funny man down with one arm and pointed to the middle of the man's back. "Sit boy, sit."

Geoffrey did his world class 'sit' in the small of the man's back. The man was totally still and the dog was totally happy. Geoffrey looked to Alphonso for approval and got it. Someone took a picture with a smart phone. Wiley was helping Alphonso up, Mary Rose was hugging Geoff and Matilda Minor-Milldew was saying, "to remain silent. You have the right..."

Geoffrey got up. People all around him were slapping Alphonso on the back and saying good things. He could tell because Alphonso was grinning as big as he, Geoff, could grin sometimes. Best of all, Geoffrey's four ladies were all hugging him and patting his neck and rubbing his ears. They needed to play this run and sit game more often.

Epilogue: Justice for All

"I didn't even get to SEE it! I didn't get to go; it was just like Corky Smith's birthday party when we were seven – I wasn't even invited!" Ken David David was depressed, disappointed and despondent.

"Ken David, if you had been here, you would have piled into the Hummer with us and we would have been glad for your help," Hadley said to reassure him.

"I didn't even get to see it," he said again. "I didn't get to help capture that Finnegan Farquhar dude. And I'm going to move to Omaha this fall. I've been accepted at Metro Community College. I was going to surprise you with that news, now I don't feel like pulling a surprise." He looked pitiful.

The girls all looked at each other, then Mary Rose jumped up and down in the big chair she was sitting in. "Ken David David, that's *wonderful!* If you move to Omaha, you can come play with Geoffrey at least three or four times a week! We can take you places in Omaha. We can be your grandmothers."

Geoffrey, lying on the floor by Ken David, who was settled in cross-legged near the couch that held Hadley and Robbie, looked up at the boy, wagged his tail and drooled as if he understood, Wiley sat in the second big chair next to Mary Rose and Alphonso was in a straight-back chair directly behind Scooter. The chief was glad to see him there. She didn't trust the kooky old lady not to run at the slightest chance.

Marge was seated in a captain's chair across from an identical chair that held the police chief. Marge's red cane was lying comfortably across her knees. Her bad knee was stretched out in front of her. Between the couch and Matilda Minor-Milldew sat a dejected and stubborn Scooter McKooter, looking more angry and vulnerable than she had since they first met her.

"Scooter," the chief said. She was still wearing her gun, her hat with the pink embroidery was tipped back on her head and her Vera Bradley bag sat obediently at her feet. "What I'm going to recommend is no jail time, but that you go to Lincoln and find an apartment in an assisted living campus where there is a memory wing."

Scooter said nothing, she just stared straight ahead. It was uncomfortable. The dolls, poem, light post and small decorative shrubs that had graced the mirrored table had been found in a black shopping bag in the pantry.

"If I understand what Finnegan Farquhar said," the chief continued, "you thought he was taking the Puritans to a reunion event then on to Scenic Point. You ordered the Puritan dolls on eBay after you learned who was coming, so you'd have the right number of men and women dolls. You wrote the poem." Matilda looked around. "But you don't remember any of that."

Scooter continued to stare straight ahead and still said nothing,

"How did you, how did she," Robbie asked, realizing that Scooter would not answer, "How did she get the poem to be so accurate? And where are the Royal Payne's? They're the only ones not accounted for."

As predicted, the Puritans registered at the B&B had returned, picked up their belongings and refused to pay their bills. They had bid the girls goodbye and shook their heads at Scooter who even then was staring straight ahead. They all hugged Mary Rose. Geoffrey got his share of attention as well. All the guests were put on alert that Chief Matilda Minor-Milldew would be calling on them.

When the chief checked the room occupied by Ophelia and Royal Payne, she found it totally cleaned out. Not one scrap of evidence remained.

"I don't know if we'll ever find the Paynes," Matilda said. "Maybe Mary Rose is right. Maybe Ophelia shot Royal during the fireworks and we'll never find her again There has been more than one body that turned to bone and dust at the bottom of one of the big silos. Corn can serve as a good, secure grave."

Going Home

They say, "All's well that ends well,"
and I'm sure that's true.

Robbie's heart had jumped out of sinus rhythm
during the chase to get Finnegan Farquhar, but it
had only lasted about half an hour then returned to
normal.

Marge's knee was, as she called it, 'a pisser,' but that's
just how life is sometimes.

Mary Rose was impressed that even during the
excitement of Finnegan Farquhar's capture she had
not needed to wear her Depends.

Wiley and Alphonso had another day of fun fishing
and had promised Brenda Lee they would come back
next year for sure.

As for Brenda Lee Colton, she purchased the bed and
breakfast from Scooter and turned it into a fabulous
staycation destination for area residents who wanted
a winter weekend away from farm and home. In
summer it was full of tourists and travelers. When
the Sandhill cranes were migrating, she had to turn
people away.

Nancy Sothanski rented one of the bedrooms from Brenda year-round. Her publisher was so excited by the Grandma Belle series that she got a huge advance and she had always wanted a writing get-away. The two women became best friends Nancy helped at the B&B and Brenda protected her writer friend's privacy like an Amazon on the warpath.

Penstemon Primrose was always welcome every afternoon and, on some really cold or bad winter days, Nancy or Brenda would go get her and drive her to the B&B for her nap. Some days, she stayed overnight, drinking tea in front of the fireplace.

The moose head watched from above, but no one ever fell asleep in it again.

The girls and their two handsome old dudes ran into Doctor Pawter at Shut Up and Drink when they went there for lunch and to say goodbye to Humiliation Strykes. She joined them for a cup of tea, since it was just after noon and her tea time. She had on her white coat and was returning from treating two stubborn old mules who had been her patients for years. She brought a massive bouquet of zinnias and greenery for Humiliation. He put them in a giant vase on the bar and that made the old tavern look elegant.

Before they left, Hadley walked the grounds looking for another feather from the red-tail hawk while the hawk itself watched her, unseen, from the top branches of the great oak tree.

The next morning, as the Hummer and trailer followed Alphonso's van out of the driveway and headed east toward Omaha, the red-tailed hawk could hear a high-pitched man's voice singing, "On the Road Again." The noise seemed to come from the black Hummer.

The hawk followed the little caravan a short way, then, circling the Hummer once, it gained some altitude and swooping into a strong current from the southwest wind, it spread its long wings and sailed gracefully and effortlessly toward the northwest horizon.

As for Scooter McKooter – she didn't go to jail, but to a very nice assisted living complex in Lincoln, Nebraska, where she became an accomplished escape artist, capturing the honor of being the oldest woman ever to shimmy down an outdoor drainpipe from the roof which ran directly next to her fourth floor apartment window.

Luckily the complex was securely fenced and gated with electronic locks. In addition, Scooter had a beautiful name tag, compliments of the judge who heard Chief Minor-Milldew's plea. Scooter loved and admired the name tag and she wore it every day. Inside the jewels was a tiny GPS which signaled her location to a fancy computer in the security office.

She didn't have a chance.

Neither did the drainpipe.

Joy Notes:

Some of you will ask about Wes Longbow's death. It was a timely one. I finished this book one month to the year after my best friend, soul mate and husband died. Marv was my Wes Longbow, the tall handsome hero in a white hat who had wisdom and grace and who loved me so much it surrounded me like the beautiful wings of a red-tailed hawk. It was only fitting that if Marv died, Wes Longbow should die, too. Their deaths were similar. The part in BOOB Girls VI when Hadley passes Wes where he sat in the big chair and says, "kiss, kiss," then presses her lips to him gently and softly, was what I did as I walked by Marv during his last few months.

Wes Longbow and Marv Johnson – two good men, and Hadley and I were lucky to have loved and been loved by them.

A Red-Tailed Hawk feather to:

Rev. Doctor James Campbell, my champion of names and ideas, who inspires me, holds my feet to the fire and makes me laugh. Jim's excellent book, *The Chair* can be purchased through Centering Corporation, as can fabulous prints of the picture of the BOOB Girl Birds on the inside back cover. Jim painted that and the big oil in my writing room is one of the best gifts I've ever gotten. Finnegan Farquhar salutes you, Slick, as does –

Butch Sleezer's Fertility Center. Jim found the sign for Butch's place in Aurelia, Iowa. My sincere thanks to Butch, Bonnie and the Boars, who gave me permission to use it and who suggested the reason for Finnegan's firing. Thanks to Sherri and everyone at the Aurelia library for inviting me to speak.

An Extra Feather to the three ladies who made generous donations to good charities in order to be characters in this book:
Nancy Sothanski is really my friend, Nancy Sothan, who, with her husband, David, have Apache Camper Centers in Bellevue, Lincoln, and Kearney, Nebraska. Nancy and Dave sold us our trailers and fifth wheel and became more than friends, they became family, people you can count on. Nancy and David were owners of Bare Essentials Clothing Optional RV Resort in *BOOB Girls III: Sandhills and Shadows,* Nancy was the coroner who explained Percolator Rasmussen's murder in *BOOB Girls IV: Murder at Meadow Lakes* and who knows who she'll be in the next mystery? In books V and VI she was simply hiding in the corners watching the action. Nancy's character was purchased at the Comfort Food Classic, supporting Ted E. Bear Hollow, Omaha area's center for grieving children. The Sothans are also generous supporters of Centering Corporation, Grief Resource Center.

Brenda Colton really does own and operate the beautiful Scenic Point Resort in Minnesota along with her husband, Terry. Her daughter and husband purchased a character for her at a live auction to raise funds for EngAge Wellness, in Omaha. The dogs in the story are really hers and Jazzmine the cat really did live and rule the roost. Brenda is a mother and a grandmother and darned good fisherman. Getting to know her was a delight and of course we had lunch at Marks Bistro in Dundee, the girls' favorite restaurant.

Jane Potter, MD, became Dr. Jane Pawter the vet thanks to two of her colleagues, Cindy Clark and Jeannie Hannan. I'm pleased she "gifted" them with doing it. Dr. Potter, if there's anything you don't like – blame them! We had fun putting her together and suffice it to say, Dr. Jane is a Creighton grad, as am I, and she has more than 100 publications to her credit. She's a geriatric doc and professor and I'm sure she can put names on the stubborn geriatric mules in the story. Che really is her dog, she raises zinnias and has flying squirrels on her farm in Iowa. She also bought her character at the EngAge Wellness fundraiser.

Mark Kurtz and **Ramon Sanchez** feed my soul at a monthly lunch where we simply talk about our work and what it means to be creative. It's real, it's laughter-filled and our one to two hours together is accurately described by Ramon as "a really good workshop."

Speaking of placing blame, let me give a red feather to my proofreaders, **Gloria Sorensen**, retired librarian and no way retired friend, and my handsome son-in-law, **Marc Roberts.** It's their fault if you find typos or is that tipoes.

Janet Roberts is not only my daughter and director of Centering Corporation; she's a genius graphic artist, putting out the Centering Catalog and *Grief Digest* Magazine as well as publishing books. She has formatted and designed the cover for this series and each one gets better.

Sheryl Fisher-Stowe, who is the new assistant manager at Meadows Lakes really IS our manager here at The Arboretum in Omaha. I have no doubt that if a rooster like Fuss N' Feathers got loose in one of our lobbies, Sheryl would catch that sucker in a minute. This is a great place to live, thanks to Sheryl's endless work and a terrific, supportive staff. Give me a call and come by – the coffee machine is literally always on.

Ruthie Lees my long-time friend and author of *Living Life with Joy in My Heart* gave me the idea for the "food police" along with a lot of laughter and support.

An old Sears catalog to **Loretta McKibben** and **Pam Allen** who contributed ideas to the Outhouse signs and donated to our remodeled bathroom at Centering Corporation.

The BOOB Girls Tour – where they've been

New additions to the tour
from this book include:

The Holland Center, where the gang went to hear the Omaha symphony Pops concert, is at 13th and Douglas, an easy walk from the heart of the Old Market. The Holland is beautiful and has perfect acoustics. Two of my grandchildren have played there with the Omaha Area Youth Orchestra.

Prospect Hill Cemetery where Anna Wilson and Dan Allen are buried is one of those best-kept secrets. Between 31st and 33rd Streets bordered by Parker and Grant Streets, the cemetery hosts a reenactment on Memorial Day. It's a delight and the location is historic and beautiful. Residents of early Omaha used to picnic there on Sundays. It's worth a visit.

Nope, I'm sorry; there isn't a Salem's Crossing, Nebraska. Ben, Centering Corporation's Development Director is Hadley's grandson who loves Highway 30 so I let him set its location. He located it to just North of **Wood River** which is two and a half hours west of Omaha just off I-80. Head there and you can see everything the girls saw and if you drive far enough, there's the **Great Platte River Road Arch, Sandhill Cranes, Grand Island** and America the Beautiful with amber waves of grain.

For the Omaha tour and tour of the other books, let's start at my own retirement community, **The Arboretum on Farnam Drive** at 8141 Farnam. The Arboretum is just east of Methodist Hospital and, if you feel ambitious, you can park somewhere nearby and walk south on 84th street to Pacific, turn right on Pacific and in a short while have coffee at **The Village Grinder.**

The Bookworm, where the girls browsed after coffee at The Grinder has moved. Get back on 84th, drive south to Center Street, turn right to 90th, right again and you're at the new location. Go in and check to see how their supply of BOOB Girl books is holding up. The Bookworm is one of the finest independent bookstores you'll ever enjoy.

There really is a **Finicky Frank's** restaurant in Omaha and it's excellent. Keisa the owner will welcome you.. It's just off of I-680 at the 30th Street exit. Go north a very short way, turn left into a short road leading to the gas station and Finicky's. My favorite thing there is the breaded pork loin.

If you are coming from West Omaha, go to 105th and Pacific,then turn south until you find the beautiful **Happy Hollow Country Club** where Hadley has taken the group in nearly every book. Unless it's lunch or dinner time, you can probably find Kelly or Jim to show you the library, the girls' favorite room.

Dorothy, who had worked at "Happy" for many years died a few years ago. The place will never be the same.

Drive on east to 72nd Street and turn left. Now you're at the area where Morgan Graves furnished La Viva Crypt from the **Lazy Leopard Lounge** auction.

Keep driving north to 72nd and Maple. Turn left and you'll be at **Centering Corporation** at 73rd Street. This is the grief resource center Joy and Dr. Marvin Johnson founded in 1977. Drive into the parking lot, come in and say hello, Inside is Caring Cups Coffee Stop. We're waiting for you. After a cup of good Joe, visit Benson Plant Rescue next door and wander through our memory garden where you will be shaded by one of the grandest and oldest cottonwoods in Nebraska.

You'll leave Centering, turn right then make a U-turn to head east again on Maple. Drive by or stop in **Jane's Health Market** and **Leo's Diner** in the village of Benson.

Continue on to 49th Street and turn right. At the corner of 49th and Happy Hollow, the house on your right – a lovely little English Tudor – belonged to Joy and Marv for more than 30 years. Keep driving and you'll be at the **Homy Inn** where the girls went for champagne on tap. As you drive across Happy Hollow, look to your right. At the end of the block, by what is lovingly called the traffic peanut, is Dan Simpson's Auto Shop. Danny found the hidden tracker in the Hummer in BOOB Girls V.

If it's near lunch time, turn right at the Homy and go to the top of the hill to 51st Street. Turn left into the village of Dundee. Park where you can and walk to **Marks Bistro,** the girls' favorite restaurant at 51st and Underwood. If the weather is nice, have lunch on the most beautiful patio in Omaha. May I suggest Mark's famous Mac and Cheese, and ask for Mark. He'll be happy to say hello, show you Joy and Marv's booth – which is also Marge and her husband's - and the table where Warren Buffett met with Hillary Clinton.

After Marks, head south on 50th Street until you come to West Center Street. Turn left on Center and drive by **Kubat Pharmacy**, one of the few remaining family-owned pharmacies and where the girls bought the bed pan for Mary Rose's bedpan hat in *BOOB Girls II.*

Continue east on Center Street and you'll come to the Old Market. Now you're on your own. Visit

Wheatfield's, The Jackson Street Tavern, M's
and of course, **Ted and Wally's Ice Cream**. Stand
beside the new Hyatt Place Hotel and look up at
the third floor of the **Mayfair Building** across 12th
Street. The apartment near the back by the fire escape
was Joy and Marv's and Robbie's. You'll be standing
where Esmeralda sang her sad song to Robbie then
patted the beautiful horse in *BOOB Girls III*. Go into
the **Passageway** where Wes and Hadley had dinner
and go smell the leather at **Overland Sheepskin**
where Wes bought a jacket. Keep walking east and
you'll come to the **ConAgr**a campus and lake.

If it's a nice day and you want to walk even more,
the **Bob Kerry** pedestrian bridge across the wide
Missouri is just a little ways north.

Enjoy a good glass of wine by turning right and
walking to the **Urban Wine Company** at 10th and
Jones. Then turn around and head west toward 15th
and Harney and **Hotel Deco**. On your way you'll
likely pass the Orpheum Theater which holds all the
grandeur from its prime.

Now drive back on Center Street to 84th Street. Turn
left on 84th and go to **Mangelsen's,** where you can
find just about everything you need, including help
making a bedpan hat.

Go south to Interstate 80 by Mangelsen's and head west. Drive to the Springfield exit and head south to Louisville. There you'll visit **Coop de Ville,** on Main Street. the neatest little gift shop ever. Walk around the corner to the big white house and explore **Feathers,** the other gift shop decorated by Dr. Liz and her ladies. Have one of Dr. Liz's Scotheroos and, like Robbie – buy a purse. It's sayings from the Coop bathroom that start the fifth book when Mary Rose looks in the mirror. "I do declare, I love my hair." That bathroom is worth a trip to Louisville anytime.

Get back on the highway by Louisville and drive a short distance to the sign reading South Bend. It's on highway 66. If it's close to dinner time, head for **Round the Bend Steakhouse,** home of the Testicle Festival. Careful. Don't miss it, it's on your left and high on a hill.

After too much food at the Bend, go north until you get to I-80 again. Head west to exit 420. There is **Pine Grove RV Resort,** former home of Marv and Joy and where the girls went on their Staycation. Come in! Have a cup of coffee. Be sure to register at the office.

Go on to **Baker's Candies** in Greenwood and shop, shop, shop at the factory store.. The gift shop is chocolate heaven.

You can dedicate an entire day to the Henry Doorly Zoo, where Marge and Alphonso had a date. I'm sorry but there is no Meadow Lakes Retirement Community. I picture it as being between Creighton University at 25th and California and the Old Market. There's no Peyton's Hair Salon, either. I picture it in one of the big apartment buildings near the river in the Old Market.

I also imagine I've left out some places. If I have, remind me and I'll add them in the next book. Enjoy!

This article was written shortly after the death of Joy's husband, Dr. Marvin Johnson
It appeared in Centering Corporation's *Grief Digest* Magazine and *Dodge Magazine* for funeral directors

I Have an Awesome Dragon and Courage is Her Name

By Joy Johnson, Co-Founder: Centering Corporation

I first noticed my dragon as I walked down the corridor of my retirement residence. It's a long corridor and as I walked I didn't know if I would open the door and find my sweet and very ill husband, Marv, alive or dead. I always worried that he would die while I was gone and he insisted on me getting out of our cheery, Disney-colored apartment for at least an hour a day and he wanted quiet alone time. No one was to come there while I was gone.

It's a long corridor.

I have time to worry.

Then all at once this dragon was there beside me.

I knew instinctively that her name was Courage.

Courage opened the door and we both went in. Everything was okay. Marv smiled his weak smile and asked me how my lunch had gone. I breathed a sigh of relief and Courage sat down beside me.

I gave the magnificent dragon a sideways glance. She was a brilliant green color with shining scales. On her big, reptilian head she wore a red helmet that stretched across her broad nose and had a silver spike attached to the center right between her eyes. Yo! This was a warrior dragon, a fighting dragon. And her tail and wings? Wow. They took up the whole apartment. There was a saddle just below her long neck that matched the helmet and by the reins I knew she was a riding dragon and I was the dragon rider, just like Eragon. She followed me everywhere. I must say she was much better at this than Margaret Thatcher, my tabby cat.

I climbed into that saddle and rode, too. The first days after Marv died I rode Courage to the funeral home to plan for his cremation and sign papers. She sat close to me. She is extremely well-behaved. She loved Marv's Celebration of Life party with nearly 300 people there and she ate an extra big piece of the cake that said, "Marv's Angel Day. March 28, 2014 (This is A Devil's Food Cake.) She ate the whole word "Devil," then burped a soft little embarrassed burp.

I rode her to a lot of "firsts". We flew – and it's a beautiful view when she's airborne and I can really feel Courage – to my first movie alone. She sat in the seat beside me. She passed on the popcorn and soda.

We flew to the mobile phone store to take Marv off my phone plan and she put her wings around me when I cried afterward because it felt as if I were deleting him. And that first really bad set of TUGS (Totally Unexpected Grief Surges) found me holding onto the tip of her wing as tight as I could. I was at the Med Center where Marv had been hospitalized way too often. I don't know if it was the time of day, the late afternoon sun coming in the windows by the escalator, or the people in the hall hurrying to go home, but all at once I felt exactly as I had years ago when we lived in our house and I was going home to be with Marv; that sweet, homey feeling of walking into love. I cried when I got to the parking garage and Courage once again wrapped me in her wings.

One time, when I had to explain to a collection agency that they had the wrong Johnson in their unkind letter, Courage looked at the agent and blew a stream of powerful flames at him. She was a fire-breathing dragon and she took no prisoners. The agent destroyed the erroneous claim.

Once while we were flying to an appointment I didn't want to keep, she turned and I took a little sign out of her mouth. It read, "Seasoned women need STDs. Strength. Tenderness. Determination and Smarts." I laughed. Courage gave me all of those in spades.

I think Courage, in her red spiked helmet; her red saddle and her brilliant scales will be with me for the rest of my life. When my time comes to die I plan to be sitting in a comfortable chair with my feet up on Courage who will be lying at my feet. Maybe she'll be in bed with me when I die. Wherever, I'm glad to have that huge wingtip to hold. I'm glad to be able to sit in her saddle and fly high, and I'm glad to know she will breathe some fire at anyone who tries to hurt me. I will have a warrior dragon every time I need one. Courage, you want half my sandwich, Girl? We're on this journey together.

Used with permission from *Grief Digest* Magazine.
www.griefdigestmagazine.com
www.centering.org

About the Author

Joy Johnson is over 75 now. With her late husband, Dr. Marvin Johnson, she founded Centering Corporation, North America's oldest and largest bereavement resource center, and Ted E. Bear Hollow, Omaha area's center for grieving children. Joy has written or edited over 100 books on grief, many for children. After she retired in 2009, she began writing **The BOOB Girls**: The Burned Out Old Broads at Table 12, a comedy-mystery series for senior women.

Joy has three children and six grandchildren. She lives in Omaha, Nebraska, with her husband, Ted Brown and a tabby cat named Margaret Thatcher. Like her characters, she is a funny, active beautiful BOOB Girl.

If you enjoy this book, you'll love and laugh with:

The Boob Girls:
The Burned Out Broads at Table 12

The Boob Girls II:
Lies, Spies and Cinnamon Roles

The Boob Girls III:
Sandhills and Shadows

The Boob Girls IV:
Murder at Meadow Lakes

The Boob Girls V:
The Secret of the Red Cane

The Boob Girls VI:
From the Eye of the Moose

The Boob Girls VII:
Ten Little Puritans

The Boob Girls VIII:
Learning to Love Willie

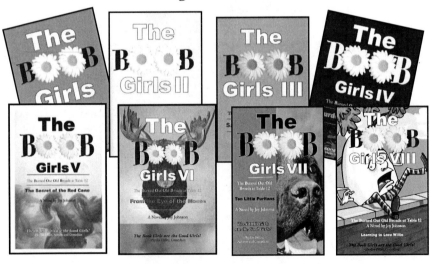

www.theboobgirls.com

Visit the girls and Joy Johnson at:

www.theboobgirls.com

The BOOB Girls are available on Kindle and Nook.

Joy is an international speaker who has presented delightful *Boob Girl* programs across the country.

Ask her about speaking at your group. You can email Joy at joy.johnson@msn.com

Other grief resources available through

www.centering.org

The BOOB Birds –

The picture on the next page is one of the best gifts I have received in my entire life.

A poem, painted by a life-time friend, Rev. Dr. James A. Campbell, all the girls are there. See if you can name them.

And get a print!

It's the best conversation piece you can ever have.

Here's what Jim says about it:
It was a daunting task. Distill the spirit of Joy Johnson and her coterie of zany, off the wall, "burned out old broads" as she calls them, into a painting. For weeks the canvas was bare. Sketch after sketch was torn up before the canvas said what it wanted to be. Animate the characters of now her several volumes of "Boob Girls" into animated birds. Still, there needed to be a context, a setting for the birds. That is when the canvas dictated an old tree with a single branch. Look closely, and one will find in the tree and the branch the first note of at least one arrangement of Beethoven's "Ode to Joy." That is the embracing truth of the painting. Within the exuberant burst of color and form is a tribute to Joy Johnson and the gift, the music, she has given the world, certainly to those most in need.
–James A. Campbell, Painter of Poems

BOOB Birds Print Full Color
Unframed, 18x24
$25

Order from www.theboobgirls.com

or

www.centering.org

Phone: 1-866-218-0101

Join Joy on Facebook at
Joy Johnson or The BOOB Girls

And sign up for the Girl's blog.
Just email Joy at joy.johnson@msn.com

For information on Joy as a
speaker for your group:
email or call: 402-639-2939

GRIEF ILLUSTRATED PRESS